VLAD the DRAC

ANN JUNGMAN

Illustrated by George Thompson

Collins

An imprint of HarperCollinsPublishers

First published in Great Britain by Dragon Books in 1982
This edition published by Collins in 1997
Collins is an imprint of HarperCollins *Publishers* Ltd
77-85 Fulham Palace Road, Hammersmith, London, W6 8JB

1 3 5 7 9 8 6 4 2

Text copyright © Ann Jungman 1982
Illustrations copyright © George Thompson 1982

ISBN 0 00 673272 0

Printed and bound in Great Britain by Caledonian International Book
Manufacturing Ltd, Glasgow G64

To Louis and Marie, with love and thanks

1
The Ravine

Judy and Paul got back into the coach – it wasn't their idea of a holiday. Three monasteries in one day! Admittedly they were painted monasteries covered with pictures from the bible hundreds of years old, and all the grown-ups seemed to think they were very splendid, but Judy and Paul agreed it was boring.

Mr and Mrs Stone had had this idea of a week's coach trip in Romania and Judy and Paul had thought it sounded good, but mostly it had been sitting in a coach.

'Well, it's only a few more days,' said Paul, 'and Mum and Dad are having a good time. Maybe we'll get a proper holiday this summer.'

'I certainly hope so,' said Judy as she settled once again in her place in the coach.

Mrs Stone leant forward. 'Don't look so miserable you two – that's our last monastery, we're going up into the mountains now and the guide says it's snowing up there, you should like that.'

Paul brightened up. 'Snow at Easter? Oh good! We'll be able to go tobogganing and sliding and build a snowman and play snowballs?'

'Well, no,' said mother. 'I doubt it, we'll just be driving through, but it'll look beautiful, the mountains are covered with pine trees with snow resting on them, it'll look like an illustration from a fairy story.'

'What's the use of snow if you can't play in it – I don't want to look at it,' grumbled Paul.

'These are no ordinary mountains,' said Mr Stone, trying to cheer the children up. 'They're the Carpathian mountains. We're travelling into Transylvania and that's vampire country. Vampires have wings and long pointed teeth that suck blood from people at night when they are asleep.'

'Really,' said Paul, 'but I thought vampires were mythical creatures that never really existed.'

'That's right,' said Mr Stone, 'but this is where the myth comes from. Count Dracula is supposed to have his castle here and we are going to visit it.'

'Was Count Dracula real then?' asked Judy.

'Well sort of,' said Mr Stone. 'You see there was a King here long long ago called King Vlad, who was very cruel and some people think the Dracula legend was based on him. But there are really no such things as vampires except in books and horror films. Still it will be exciting to see the Carpathian mountains and the castles don't you think?'

'I'd rather go tobogganing,' grumbled Paul, 'but it'll be better than monasteries I suppose.'

As the coach climbed higher and higher into the mountains, even Paul and Judy were impressed by

8

the scenery. The mountains seemed to touch the sky and though it was cold the sun was shining and the snow glistened silver on the trees. After a few hours' drive they came to a spectacular ravine, the rocky sides of the mountain rose up sheer on either side of a narrow path. It was dramatic, frightening and beautiful.

'I can just imagine bandits operating round here,' said Paul.

'What a spot for an ambush.'

Lots of people in the coach wanted to take photographs, so the coach stopped.

'Be back in ten minutes,' said the guide.

'Can we go for a walk in the snow?' asked Paul.

'Of course,' said Mr Stone, 'but be careful you don't get left behind.'

'No fear,' said Judy. 'Not here, it's really creepy. I'd be scared stiff alone here, and at night I think I'd just die of terror.'

'Off you go then,' said Mrs Stone.

Paul and Judy got off the coach and looked up in amazement at the steep rugged sides of the ravine.

'It really is strange isn't it?' said Judy. 'Not at all real, more like a picture from an old book.'

At that moment a snow-ball hit the back of her neck and the water trickled down.

'That wasn't fair,' she shouted at Paul. 'I wasn't ready,' and she picked up a handful of snow to make into a snowball. Paul dashed off down the path. After a minute he slipped and fell. He sat up

9

quickly but Judy leapt on top of him and stuffed snow down his coat. They were rolling in the snow and laughing when a voice said indignantly,

'Do you mind, you're crushing me.'

'Did you say something Judy?' asked Paul.

'No,' said Judy. 'I thought you did.'

'Oh, stop whittering on and get up,' yelled the same voice, 'I'm suffocating.'

The two children leapt up and there under the stone that Paul had dislodged sat a tiny creature with a comical face, two long pointed teeth, long ears and a hurt expression.

'That's better,' said the tiny creature. 'I thought my last hour had come. I don't know what you two think you're doing,' it continued disapprovingly. 'I've been sleeping peacefully under that stone for a hundred years and now you come barging in without so much as a by your leave. No manners if you ask me!'

Judy and Paul were speechless with amazement. Eventually Paul said 'I'm not imagining this am I, Judy?'

'No, I can see and hear it, too. I wonder what it is?'

'I'm a baby vampire,' said the little thing indignantly. 'I'd have thought you'd know that.'

'How could we?' replied Paul. 'We've never seen a vampire, and my Dad says they don't exist.'

'That's silly,' said the baby vampire angrily. 'Of course I exist, though I begin to think I may be the last of the vampires,' he added sadly. 'And if you'd

had anything to do with it, I would have been.'

'I'm so sorry we squashed you,' said Judy. We didn't mean to. Please tell us about yourself. It's so exciting to meet a real vampire. You're not dangerous are you? Dad says vampires suck blood.'

'Talking of blood,' interrupted Paul, 'he may try to suck mine. Look at my knee. I cut it on that stone when I fell over.'

The children heard a moan and looked over to see the vampire keel over and lie on his back.

'I think the poor little thing has fainted,' said Judy. 'I'll put some snow on his face.'

'Do you think it's a good idea?' mused Paul. 'He really might be dangerous.'

'Oh, Paul, we woke him up after his long sleep. We can't just leave him, he may have fainted because he's not used to the air.'

So Judy put some snow on the vampire's face while Paul cleaned up his knee with his hankie. After a moment the vampire began to moan and then opened his eyes.

'Has the blood gone?'

'Yes,' said Judy.

'I told you he was after blood,' said Paul. 'Come on, let's get out of here.'

'Why did you faint?' asked Judy.

'Promise you won't tell,' said the baby vampire looking tearful.

'Of course,' said Judy. 'Go on Paul promise.'

'Oh, all right,' muttered Paul dubiously.

'Well, the truth is I'm a very bad vampire. I faint at the sight of blood,' confessed the vampire, blushing and looking at his feet. 'In fact, I'm a vegetarian. I was a terrible disappointment to my mother,' he sobbed, 'so she put me under the stone while they tried to decide what to do with me. I've been under there for a hundred years' (except for the time I went to Great Uncle Ghitza's funeral) with no one to talk to,' and he burst into tears again.

'Oh you poor little thing,' said Judy and picked him up and stroked the top of his head.

'Watch it,' said Paul.

'Oh, he's harmless,' said Judy, 'he's just sad and lonely.'

'Yes I am,' wept the vampire. Then he looked pleadingly at Judy.

'Would you take me back to England with you?'

'We can't take you back to England,' said Paul.

'Why not?' said Judy. 'People would love him.'

'That's right,' said the vampire. 'I know I'd get on well with the English. Whenever coaches come to my ravine I wake up and listen to the conversation. That's how my English is so good. The English are really interested in vampires. London is in England isn't it?'

'Yes,' said Judy. 'We live in London.'

'Well, they make films there about vampires, don't they?' said the vampire importantly. 'I thought maybe I could become a film star. What do you think?'

13

'Well, you're a bit small,' mused Judy.

'I'll grow, if I find some food,' said the vampire. 'Please, please take me to London. I'm so bored and lonely here in the ravine.'

'P-a-u-l, J-u-d-y, hurry up. The whole coach is waiting for you. Whatever are you doing?'

'Coming!' yelled Judy. 'We've got to go now,' she said to the vampire.

'Shall we put you back under your stone?'

'Oh, please take me with you, please, please, I'll be very good. I'll do anything you say. Please don't leave me all alone. I like you both, we'll have lovely times. How would you like to live under that stone?'

'JUDY, PAUL, come on!'

The vampire looked up at Judy and Judy looked at Paul. Poor Paul, he had never been as daring as his sister. But he also couldn't bear to hurt any living creature. He looked down at the pathetic little monster, hesitated for a second, then bent down and picked him up.

'It's all your fault, Judy,' he said, as he shoved the vampire into his pocket and dashed back to the coach, followed by Judy.

'Whatever were you two doing?' asked Mrs Stone. 'We called and called.'

'We just went for a walk,' said Judy.

'We almost went without you,' said Mr Stone. 'You'd have liked that wouldn't you? Alone in the mountains, with vampires creeping up on you.'

'Don't be silly, Dad. There's no such thing as vampires.'

Paul heard a muffled chuckle coming from his pocket.

2

What's in a Name?

When the coach arrived at the hotel it was already dark.

'Be downstairs for supper in five minutes,' said Mrs Stone.

Judy and Paul dashed up to their hotel room and locked the door. Paul got the vampire out of his pocket and put him on the bed. The vampire looked round the room and sniffed. 'What's this place?'

'It's a room in a hotel, we're only staying here one night. You'll have to stay here now and keep quiet, and out of sight. We've got to go and have supper, but we'll come back as soon as we can.'

'What about me?' said the vampire indignantly. 'I'm hungry.'

'Well, we'll bring you up some food if we can.'

'Oh, all right,' grumbled the vampire, 'but don't forget that I'm a vegetarian.'

At supper the children stuffed bits of cheese and apple and sugar and tomato into their pockets. As soon as supper was over they said they were terribly tired and dashed off to their room.

When they got back the vampire was nowhere to be seen.

'Do you think he's escaped?' asked Judy anxiously.

'Wouldn't it be dreadful if he did something vampirish while we were looking after him?' commented Paul.

'It's all right, here I am,' called the vampire and stuck his head out from between the curtains.

'Whatever are you doing there?' asked Paul.

'Was scared,' confessed the vampire. 'Is that food? Caw, jolly good, I'm starving.'

The vampire tried the cheese and pulled a face. 'Ugh, that's horrible,' he complained, and rejected the apple, the sugar and the tomato equally emphatically.

'Oh, dear,' said Judy, 'I've no idea what vegetarian vampires like to eat.'

'I suppose I'll just have to starve as usual,' muttered the vampire looking sorry for himself.

'Don't worry baby vampire,' said Judy soothingly, 'we'll think of something. By the way what's your name, we can't keep on calling you vampire.'

'I haven't got one,' said the vampire sadly. 'I never did have a name 'cos Great Uncle Ghitza wouldn't come to my christening on account of my being a vegetarian and a disgrace to the vampires.'

'Who's Great Uncle Ghitza?' asked Paul.

'You haven't heard of my Great Uncle Ghitza?' asked the vampire in a shocked tone. 'Why he was the wickedest of all the vampires, even the other vampires were scared of Great Uncle Ghitza. He was my Great Uncle, my Grandfather Nicolai's

17

brother,' explained the vampire glowing with pride. 'You can be jolly glad I'm not my Great Uncle Ghitza, he'd have vampirised you both by now.'

'Oh,' said Paul, 'well then I'm glad it's you we're talking to and not him, but that still doesn't solve the problem of your name.'

'Well you make a suggestion,' said the vampire, 'and I'll tell you what I think of it.'

'Timothy,' said Judy. 'That's a nice name and we could always shorten it to "Tim" or "Timmy".'

The vampire gave her a withering look. 'Don't be silly,' he said, 'I can't have an English name.'

'Well I don't know any Romanian names except for the Kings like Carol and Michael.'

'You don't understand, you don't understand me one bit. I don't want an ordinary name, I want a vampiry name, something to scare people silly, that'll make them quake in their boots and shake and tremble.'

'But you're not a bit frightening,' laughed Judy.

'Exactly,' said the vampire, 'so it's all the more important that I have a scary name. A real creepy, spine-chilling vampire name.'

'Honestly you do expect a lot,' complained Paul. 'How could we know about vampire names. Let's see, there was that King Dad told us about, Vlad the Impaler and then there's Count Dracula himself, of course.'

'King Vlad – Count Dracula mmmmmmmm!' The vampire thought hard. 'I've got it – Vlad the

Drac! Yes that's what I'll be called, Vlad the Drac.' He smiled. 'That'll make them quiver at the knees and jibber with fear won't it? I like it, yes I do like it. Vlad the Drac, it's perfect. Don't you think it's good?' he asked the children.

'Well if it's what you want we'll call you Vlad,' agreed Paul and Judy.

'Of course it's what I want,' said the vampire happily. 'If I could only have some decent food I'd be a very happy vampire.'

'You mustn't worry about that little Vlad, we'll find something you like.'

Vlad looked at her, appalled, and stamped his foot. 'You called me little Vlad,' he said in an aggrieved tone. 'You may call me Vlad the Bold, or Vlad the Bad, or Vlad the Wise, or Vlad the Beau-tiful, or Vlad the Fierce, or Vlad the Brave or Prince Vlad, or Lord Vlad or Judge Vlad, or King Vlad or Emperor Vlad, or Chairman Vlad, or Pope Vlad, or Dr Vlad or even Professor Vlad, but not, I repeat not *little* Vlad!'

'All right,' giggled Judy, 'we'll remember.' Paul sighed with relief that the tirade was over.

'Now,' said Vlad, 'now that I've got a name and everything, you tell me what all the things in this room are. I've never seen a room like this – things have changed in a hundred years. Progress and that. I've been blowing on that big round candle but it won't go out. It doesn't even flicker.'

'Because it's not a candle,' said Paul. 'It's an electric light.'

'What's electric?' said Vlad.

'Well you just push a switch and you get light like you used to get from candles and gas lamps in the old days,' said Paul. 'Electricity generates heat, too – those radiators are worked by electricity.'

Vlad touched one of the radiators gingerly and withdrew his hand quickly.

'Ooo! it's very hot, well, well, the wonders of modern science. Great Uncle Ghitza didn't approve of progress, he thought it would be bad for vampires and he was right. What's that thing there?'

'That's a telephone, it's for talking to people.'

But before Paul could finish his explanation, Vlad leapt under a pillow and was trembling violently.

'What's the matter with you Vlad?' asked Judy.

'How could you, how could you put me in a room with one of these things,' wept Vlad still trembling.

'But why are you so frightened of a telephone?'

'It was one of those things that was the end of poor Great Uncle Ghitza.'

'Don't be silly, no one, least of all a vampire could be killed by a telephone.'

'Well he was. Poor Uncle Ghitza, they tried all the usual ways to kill a vampire, stakes at cross roads at midnight, church chimes and all that, crypts and garlic and crosses, but Great Uncle was too tough for them until he fell foul of a telephone. He was trying to pull one of those "infernal machines" as he called them away from a wall when he got caught in the wire and strangled himself.'

'Well it serves him right,' said Judy. 'He sounds like a nasty piece of work. Now Vlad you just try to forget about the telephone. No harm will come to you. Come on we'll go and have a look at the bathroom.'

'All right,' snuffled Vlad in a small voice and clung pathetically to Judy's collar while casting accusing looks at the telephone. Looking round the tiled bathroom Vlad asked, 'What's that?'

'That's a bath,' said Judy. 'You fill it with warm water and then wash yourself in it.'

'Oh I don't like the sound of that,' said Vlad.

'It's quite nice,' Paul reassured him.

'Is it? Can I have a bath then?' asked Vlad.

'Why not,' said Judy, 'but we'd better bathe you in the basin since you're so small.'

So they filled the basin and Vlad stood on the edge looking anxious.

'Try the water with your big toe and see if it's the right temperature,' said Judy.

Vlad gingerly put his big toe in the water. 'Too hot,' he complained. So some more cold water was added.

'Too cold,' grumbled the vampire. 'Changed my mind – don't think I'll have a bath after all,' and he got up to walk away, slipped on a piece of soap and fell into the basin s-p-l-a-s-h!

'What happened?' gasped Vlad, when he surfaced.

'You slipped on some soap.'

'What's soap?'

'Stuff you clean yourself with – like this.'

Vlad looked at the soap, looked at it, sniffed and then to the children's amazement took a huge bite.

'Delicious,' he said. 'This is what Vlad really likes,' and he demolished the whole bar of soap in one minute.

'I don't think much of baths,' he confided in Judy as she dried him, 'but soap is smashing.'

'I don't much like baths, myself,' said Judy. 'But the thought of eating soap is disgusting.'

'Well, it's a problem solved for us,' said Paul. 'Vlad can eat your bar of soap in each hotel for breakfast and you can stay as dirty as you like. But you'll have to keep your teeth out of my soap, Vlad. I like to keep myself clean.'

'That's all right,' said Vlad happily, 'I won't touch yours. Now I've got a name and a diet I'll be very well behaved. Though I think you ought to change your mind about your soap. Eating's much more fun than washing and the taste may grow on you.'

3

Home

The holiday passed and it was time to go home.

Paul and Judy enjoyed Vlad's company and he certainly improved the last part of the trip. On the day they were due to leave Judy explained to Vlad.

'Look Vlad, today we're going to take the plane back to London. Now you must have a long think, are you sure you want to come home with us?'

'Course I'm sure,' said Vlad happily. 'I want to be a film star and anyway I like you. This is much more fun than being under a stone.'

'You'll have to go on a plane you know.'

'What's a plane?'

'Oh dear, how do you explain a plane – well it's like a coach but its got wings and can fly in the air.'

'Oh, I see, like a vampire.'

'Well, sort of.'

'Paul,' said Judy, 'how are we going to get Vlad through customs – they search very carefully since all these hi-jackings?'

'What happens if I get caught,' asked Vlad.

'We'll all be in trouble,' said Paul, with a worried frown. 'We'll all be arrested and you'll be put in a zoo or a museum so you mustn't get caught. How can we hide him, Judy?'

'We'll pretend he's a souvenir,' said Judy triumphantly.

'What's a souvenir?' asked Vlad looking suspicious.

'Something you take home from holiday to remind you of your holiday,' explained Judy.

'But that's what I am,' said Vlad.

'Yes, but souvenirs aren't usually alive.'

'I'll pretend that I'm not alive, I'll pretend to be a pretend vampire.'

'That's a good idea,' said Judy, 'but you'll have to be very still.'

'I won't even blink,' Vlad assured her.

Next day they were at the airport. Vlad put his head out of Paul's pocket as a jet passed over. 'Terrible noise,' he commented loudly, 'and what an awful lot of people.'

'Shut up,' said Paul nervously. 'From now on don't say a word. Judy can you take him, please, he's your souvenir.'

Judy took Vlad who looked around curiously at everything.

'Do stop moving about,' worried Paul.

'Where's the plane?' asked Vlad, trying to stay still.

'Be quiet,' hissed Judy fiercely, 'and don't you dare move your head again.'

'Passports ready, you two,' said Mr Stone as they went through to the departure lounge.

Paul trembled as the man turned the pages of first his passport, and then Judy's. He dared not

look at Vlad. It was even worse going through the security check. Judy had to put Vlad down with her bag to be searched while she went through the metal detector arch. Paul was as terrified as Vlad, as he watched the security man decide whether or not a toy vampire might be concealing a danger-ous weapon.

'What was that in aid of,' said Vlad once he was safely back with Judy.

'It's to stop terrorists hi-jacking the plane,' explained Judy.

'They hold the crew at knifepoint or gunpoint and take over the plane,' said Paul.

'Sounds a lot worse than anything a vampire ever did,' said Vlad smugly.

'Be quiet,' whispered Judy. 'It's still not safe. Don't say a word until we're on the plane and you're back in Paul's pocket.

'Is that a plane?' asked Vlad. 'Don't want to go on it. No I don't. Don't like the look of that big vampiry thing at all.'

'Well, would you prefer to be left alone here at Bucharest airport then?' asked Judy.

'No, don't leave me,' whimpered Vlad.

'Then be quiet,' snapped Judy, 'and do as you're told.'

Vlad enjoyed the flight, peering out of the window, watching the smoking and seat belt signs going on and off, and keeping up a running commentary. Fortunately the engine noise was loud enough to drown his cheerful chatter; and he managed to snuggle under Judy's seat belt every time a steward went by. Paul brought him a little tablet of soap from the toilet and all went well until they landed and he had to be quiet again.

Judy gave Vlad to Paul to put in his pocket, because she had to help her mother carry the presents she'd bought on the plane.

'Anything to declare, you two,' said Mr Stone as they went through customs. 'Haven't brought back any vampires, have you?'

Paul went white as the customs man looked in to his eyes. He knew he had guilt written all over his face. But Vlad stayed still and Judy smiled so innocently as she went past, that the customs man patted her on the head and grinned at her brother.

'Thank heavens that's over,' sighed Paul as they waited for a taxi.

'I knew it would be all right, Paul,' said Judy. 'You worry too much.'

So eventually Vlad arrived at 7 Willow Gardens, N.W.5. The children took Vlad for a tour of the house and explained what everything was for.

'That's our bedroom,' said Judy. 'You can sleep in the top drawer of Paul's chest of drawers one night and the top drawer of mine the next.'

'I see,' said Vlad, 'perfectly suitable for an aristocratic vampire. I'd hate to be in a lower drawer.

'Ha, ha,' groaned Paul.

'What happens during the day?' enquired Vlad.

'Well on weekdays we have to go to school,' said Paul, 'so you'll have to be good and stay quietly in the drawer. If you get caught you'll be in trouble and so will we. So whatever happens you mustn't get out of the drawer when we aren't there.'

'I'll be good,' vowed Vlad. 'Now – show me the rest of the house.'

'Remember, whatever happens you are never, never to wander around the house during the day,' Paul stressed. 'Dad's at home a lot and if he catches you we'll have to answer a lot of jolly difficult questions!'

'Why is your father at home a lot?' asked Vlad. 'Hasn't he got a job?'

'Yes, he has but he's a violinist, so he doesn't work all the time. He has to stay at home to practise so he looks after us, while Mum goes out to work. Dad'll be famous one day.'

'What does your mother do?' asked Vlad.

'She's a doctor. She works at the hospital,' said Judy. 'She has to work very hard.'

'A lady doctor!' exclaimed Vlad, 'well, well, there's progress for you. My goodness, she must be a very clever lady. Though, Great Uncle Ghitza would never approve – a lady doctor, ummmm. Still, I think it's very good your Mum being a doctor whatever Great Uncle Ghitza would have said, real progress.'

'Anyway, Vlad, that's the situation, so you stay quietly in the drawer while we're at school.'

'Oh, all right,' groaned Vlad. 'But it doesn't

sound much better than being under my stone.'

'Now this is the kitchen,' said Judy, brightly changing the subject. 'This is where we cook and wash up and things.'

'I see,' said Vlad, and went off and investigated everything thoroughly. 'What a lot of interesting things. This is a bit like the basin I fell into.'

'Yes, it's a sink for washing dishes and clothes, but not vampires.'

'I see, and what is this?'

'Washing-up liquid,' answered Paul. 'Why?'

'Think I'll just have a little taste,' explained the vampire and he sank his little fangs into the plastic bottle. 'Ummmm,' he exclaimed smacking his lips, 'super, delicious, even better than soap. I think I'd prefer to have washing-up liquid in future.'

'Oh, look what you've done,' squealed Judy. 'All the liquid will seep through those holes. Mum will be bound to notice.'

'He's going to be far too much trouble,' said Paul. 'I think we should take him to the police and pretend he stowed away in our luggage.'

'We could take him to the zoo,' said Judy.

'You promised, you promised, you promised, you'd look after me. You can't do that to poor Vlad,' whimpered Vlad.

'Well don't stick your fangs in things,' said Judy, 'and stop whining.'

So Vlad stopped whining and Mrs Stone thought she must have speared the washing-up liquid on a fork. All was well for a few days. But life with Vlad was not easy. The children spent all their pocket money on washing-up liquid. They worried about being caught and Vlad complained about the boredom of his life in the drawers.

'How would you like to be left sitting in a drawer all on your own all day,' he grumbled, 'particularly with him, the phantom fiddler screeching away down below,' and Vlad began to imitate a violin.

'Don't talk about my father like that,' snapped Judy. 'He's going to be a great violinist.'

'Well from where I'm sitting it certainly doesn't sound like it,' replied Vlad rudely.

'Don't go on so,' said Paul, 'school isn't that exciting either you know.'

'Swop you,' offered Vlad. 'You sit in the drawer listening to that horrible noise and I'll go to school.'

'Don't be silly,' yelled both the children.

But really they were worried about Vlad during the day. The vampire was getting very restless. One afternoon when they got home from school Vlad was in neither drawer. They rushed round the house calling his name. They looked everywhere.

'Shh!' said Judy, 'I think I can hear something.'

A low moan was coming from the laundry cupboard.

'The laundry cupboard!' said Judy, and rushed to open it. And sure enough there lay Vlad moaning and groaning and clutching his stomach.

31

'Oh dear,' said Judy. 'He looks awful, he must be ill.'

'Ohhh,' shrieked Vlad, 'ill, sick, dying. That bottle of washing-up liquid was poisoned. Ohhhh!'

Judy looked at the bottle.

'Special lemon added,' she read. 'Oh poor Vlad, the lemon obviously disagrees with him. Maybe we should ring mother's surgery.'

Vlad stopped moaning. 'A lady doctor. Don't you dare bring a lady doctor anywhere near me.'

'But Vlad I thought you approved of lady doctors. You said you did.'

'Never mind what I said, I won't have a lady doctor near me. I'd rather die.'

'Judy, if he's going to carry on like this, we'd better give him some of that medicine Mum gives us when we get stomach aches,' said Paul and rushed off to fetch it.

'Here Vlad,' said Judy when Paul returned with the bottle and a spoon, 'have a spoonful of this.'

But Vlad grabbed the bottle, swallowed the whole lot and then said, rubbing his tummy, 'that was nice, I feel better already. Is there any more?'

4
Vlad gets Vampirish

One afternoon Paul and Judy arrived home from school and as usual went straight up to the bedroom to find Vlad.

'He's not up here,' called Judy from her room. 'Is he with you Paul?'

'No,' called Paul. 'He must have gone exploring, we'd better find him before Mum or Dad come home. Vlad, where are you?'

There was no answer. The children looked in the bathroom, and in their parents' bedroom and then in the front room.

'He's gone,' said Paul.

'We haven't looked in the kitchen yet.'

'But we've told him he mustn't go in there.'

'Well maybe he got hungry and went into the kitchen to find something to eat.'

'I suppose we'd better check,' said Paul.

So they went to look in the kitchen and when they opened the door, sure enough, there on the kitchen table sat Vlad looking very pleased with himself and singing:

> 'Oh my name's Vlad the Drac,
> And my deeds are so black,
> Tra, la, la, la, la, la, laaaaa.'

'Vlad, what are you doing down here? You know perfectly well that you're supposed to be upstairs.'

'Don't talk to me like that, young man,' replied Vlad. 'I'll go wherever I please.'

'Vlad, what have you been up to?'

'I've been vampirish,' replied Vlad and clacked his teeth at the children.

'Paul, look,' said Judy, turning pale, 'there's blood all over the kitchen.'

Paul was white faced and backing towards the door.

'Oh no! Judy it's true. Maybe he's turned into a real vampire after all. Whatever shall we do?'

Vlad sat humming, unperturbed. He licked the blood off his long nails, smacked his lips and said, 'Ummm, delicious.'

'Now Vlad,' said Judy sternly, 'you're to tell us exactly what has happened. Where did all that blood come from?'

'I don't mind telling you one bit,' said Vlad amiably. 'It's very simple. I, just as Great Uncle Ghitza would have done, ate the milkman.'

'You ate the milkman! I can't believe it. How terrible. Why did you eat the milkman?'

'Oh, I don't know, I suppose vampires will be vampires. I just felt terribly hungry and then the milkman called, so I ate him, it's quite logical.'

'If you ate the milkman, where's his crate?' demanded Judy.

'Oh, I ate that too. I had this terrible hunger.

Mind you I found that crate a bit indigestible, not as bad as the bucket and dishcloth. That dishcloth was disgusting. Yuck!'

'What dishcloth, what bucket? Milkmen don't have buckets.'

'Oh, I forgot to tell you. The window cleaner called afterwards and I was still hungry so I ate him too.'

'You ate the window cleaner?' asked Judy faintly.

'Yes,' said Vlad. 'Can't tell a lie, I did.'

'Oh, Paul,' said Judy looking pale, 'what have we done, bringing this monster back from Transylvania? How will we ever explain to the police and Mum and Dad about this? The milkman *and* the window cleaner!'

'And the gas man,' added Vlad smugly.

'What?' yelled Paul from behind the door.

'Him too?' asked Judy in disbelief.

'Oh, yes,' said Vlad. 'Well he came to read the meter and I was still peckish so I ate him too. He was a bit skinny and tough, though, I didn't enjoy him much.'

'This is awful,' groaned Paul.

'I feel sick,' muttered Judy.

'You can feel jolly glad I'm not still hungry,' said Vlad, 'or I'd eat you too,' and he clacked his teeth.

'But what about the mess? We shall have to clear it up. And Mum and Dad will have to know. They'll never believe us, they'll think we've gone mad,' said Judy. She extracted a promise from Vlad that he wouldn't harm them. Then Paul came back in the kitchen and helped Judy mop up the mess, while Vlad sang happily:

> 'Oh I'm Vlad the Drac,
> And my deeds are so black.'

Suddenly Judy called:

'Paul – look here!'

'What have you found, some bones or something?'

'No,' said Judy, 'only a broken bottle of tomato ketchup.'

The children stared at the splodgy red mess for a moment, then they rounded on the little vampire. 'Vlad, you just come here and explain yourself.'

Vlad was sliding down the table leg. He waved his hand and began to walk towards the door.

'You'll excuse me, I was just going for a walk.'

'Oh no you're not, you just come back here and explain why you made up all that nonsense about eating the milkman and the window cleaner and the gas man and giving us the fright of our lives.'

Vlad looked very small and began to whimper, 'I just wanted to feel like a real vampire, just once in my life, just once I wanted to be scary like Great Uncle Ghitza. You don't know what it's like to be a vampire who never scared anyone.'

'Well it's no excuse for frightening us like that. We've done our best for you and look how you behave. Now you just sit down and be quiet and feel guilty while we decide what to do with you.'

'Poor old Vlad, poor little Drac,' muttered Vlad and sat with his head in his hands and looked out of the window. 'Poor old Vlad, poor little Drac.'

'Shut up,' snapped Paul. 'We don't want another word out of you. Judy I'm starving, did Mum leave us anything to eat?'

'There's a note here,' answered Judy. 'If you are hungry there is a shepherd's pie in the oven, love Mum.'

'Great. I'll put the oven on and heat it up.'

A quarter of an hour later the children were happily eating the pie.

Vlad looked at them accusingly.

'What I want to know,' said Vlad. 'What I want to know is why it is all right for you to eat shepherd's pie if I can't eat milkmen and window cleaners not in a pie?'

'Oh, Vlad,' laughed Judy. 'You are funny.'

'Don't be nice to him,' said Paul. 'He's in disgrace.'

'Oh, just let me explain. Vlad,' said Judy, 'this pie hasn't got a shepherd in it, it's a pie made from mince meat and potatoes that shepherds like to eat!'

'Umm,' said Vlad dubiously. 'I wouldn't be too sure about that if I were you, all that white stuff on the top looks like wool. Invites suspicion if you ask me.'

'Oh, Vlad, do stop,' cried Judy. 'You're putting me off my supper.'

'Yes, go upstairs, you nasty little thing,' said Paul. 'We've had enough of you.'

'Poor old Vlad, poor little Drac,' sighed Vlad. 'When I wanted to go for a walk they made me come back, I can't do anything right. Poor old Vlad, poor little Drac. Wish I'd stayed under my nice comfortable stone,' and he walked away muttering loudly. 'Take me from under my nice cosy stone and then treat me like this. It's not right. Great Uncle Ghitza would never have put up with it,' and he slammed the kitchen door indignantly.

'Don't worry about him Paul,' said Judy. 'He'll get over it.'

'He must learn to behave,' said Paul, 'or we'll worry every day when we have to leave him to

go to school.'

'I suppose so,' said Judy, 'but poor little chap, it must be very boring for him.' She could still hear mutterings of 'Poor old Vlad, poor little Drac' as he climbed the stairs.

A few days later Paul and Judy came home to be greeted by loud singing.

'For tonight we'll merry, merry be,' rang out a voice. 'Tomorrow I'll be sober.'

'That's never Dad,' said Paul. 'It must be Vlad.' They both dashed into the kitchen where the noise came from, and sure enough there was Vlad lying in the butter, with an empty bottle of sherry lying next to him. He giggled when he saw the children.

'Vlad,' they shouted. 'What have you been doing?'

'Taking my medicine,' laughed Vlad.

'Get up out of the butter,' shouted Paul.

'No need to shout old chap,' said Vlad amiably and got up from the butter and tripped and fell headlong into the sugar.

Judy pulled him out. 'Vlad, you're drunk,' she said reproachfully.

Vlad just smiled at her in a vague happy way.

'You'd better take him away and bath him,' said Paul. 'He's disgusting. Look at him covered in butter and sugar. I'll clean up the mess he's made down here.'

So Judy washed Vlad and tried to quieten down his singing and then put him in her drawer where he fell into a deep sleep. Late that night Judy was woken by someone whispering her name.

'Judy, Judy wake up.'

'Oh, Vlad it's late and I was asleep, what is it?'

'I feel sick.'

'Well, it's not surprising. You got drunk and now you've got a hangover.'

'Well, why doesn't it go and hang over someone else?' complained Vlad. 'Judy I'm sorry I got drunk, I didn't mean to, I thought it was that lovely medicine you gave me when I had a bad tummy. I don't like being drunk.'

'Well it was sherry you were drinking. Next time read the label on the bottle. Now go back to sleep and please, please stop wandering round the house.'

'I promise I won't get drunk again,' said Vlad fervently, 'and I'll never, never wander round the house again.'

Judy heaved a sigh of relief and went to sleep, contented.

5
The Curse of the Vampire

Vlad stuck to his word. Not once did he venture out during the day. He stayed in the drawer and listened to the radio that Paul thoughtfully remembered to forget to turn off. The children's homecoming was the highlight of the little vampire's day.

'Hello,' said Vlad cheerfully one day as the children opened the drawer and let him out. 'Guess what I did today while you were at school?'

'What did you do?' asked Judy.

'I made up a vampire song,' said Vlad proudly. 'I heard a hippopotamus song on the radio and I decided that there ought to be a vampire song, so I made one up all on my own. Would you like to hear it?'

'Yes,' said the children.

So Vlad went and stood on the window sill, cleared his throat and began:

'Blood, blood, glorious blood,
Nothing quite like it for mixing with mud.
So follow me, follow me,
Down your neck's hollow,
And there let us swallow some glorious blood.'

'It's horrid,' said Judy.

'Blood-thirsty,' said Paul.

'Well, of course it's blood-thirsty,' answered Vlad indignantly. 'It's a vampire song, I don't know what you expect, "Here we go round the Mulberry bush" or "Shine on Harvest Moon". You seem to forget that I'm a vampire,' and Vlad sat down disconsolately, sighed deeply and looked out of the window.

'Sorry Vlad,' said Judy. 'You were very clever to make up that song even if it is a bit gruesome.'

'Jolly well was clever. Am clever,' agreed Vlad.

'Hey Judy,' said Paul, 'look, here it says that there's going to be a film on TV tonight called "The Curse of the Vampire". I wish we could watch that!'

'Caw, so do I,' said Vlad. 'Would your Mum and the phantom fiddler let us watch?'

'No,' said Judy gloomily. 'They never let us watch horror films.'

Vlad looked tearful. 'I must see it, I just must. I expect Great Uncle Ghitza is in it. Think of a way for us to see it, oh please, please. I'll be good for ever and ever if you promise to find a way.'

'Well we can always ask,' said Paul, 'but I wouldn't give much for our chances. Come on Judy, let's go and ask.'

So the children trooped off downstairs and Vlad went and stood on the landing, his head stuck between the banisters straining to hear.

'Mum, can Judy and I watch television tonight?

43

There's a film on we particularly want to see.'

'What film's that?' asked Mrs Stone.

'It's about vampires,' said Paul. 'Ever since we went to Romania we've had a special interest in them. In fact Judy and I are both doing projects at school on vampires, so we really do need to see this film for educational reasons.'

'Is it a horror film?' asked Mrs Stone.

'Well some people might think so,' said Paul. 'But not for people like me, doing a study of vampires. That side of it wouldn't interest me.'

'Well, I'm not sure,' said Mrs Stone.

'You see Dad is playing in a concert tonight and I'm going to hear him. Mrs Fitzwilliams is coming in to baby-sit.'

'Baby-sit!' said Paul and Judy indignantly. 'Honestly Mum, it's just daft – we're not babies. We'll be all right on our own. You won't be back that late.'

'Yes, but if you do stay alone, I'm not sure I want you watching films on vampires. You'll be up all night insisting you've got vampires in your room or something.'

'Oh Mum, please – you owe us a treat 'cos we're not going to Dad's concert. Let us stay and watch and leave Mrs Fitzwilliams' number. We'll ring her if we feel scared, or there's a fire or anything.'

'You'll never get up for school in the morning if you stay up that late,' said their mother, half-heartedly searching for reasons why they shouldn't watch the film.

'It's Friday,' chorused the children triumphantly.

'Oh all right,' said Mrs Stone. 'I haven't got time to argue but if you have nightmares about vampires I'll be very annoyed.'

'We're not scared of vampires,' said Paul. 'My experience of vampires is that they're misunderstood, they're quite sweet really.'

'Well let's hope you never meet one, you might change your mind. Anyway when Dad and I come home we want to find the two of you in bed – is it a bargain?'

'Yes, Mum,' chorused the children.

So later that evening Judy and Paul were sitting on the couch looking at the television, clasping mugs of cocoa, while Vlad sat on the arm of the couch with a thimble full of medicine as a special treat.

'When does the film start?' asked Vlad, 'I'm ever so excited.'

'Not for a while, it's "Sportsnews" first,' said Paul.

'Oh,' said Vlad despondently, 'I don't want to see that, I'm only interested in "The Curse of the Vampire".'

'Well, you'll just have to wait,' said Paul, 'and be quiet because I want to know the line up for tomorrow's match.'

'Sport's boring,' grumbled Vlad, as the programme started. 'It's silly, us vampires don't bother with sport.'

'Shut-up,' yelled both the children.

'Poor old Vlad, poor little Drac,' complained the vampire.

'Why are those two men hitting each other?' he asked.

'It's called boxing,' explained Paul patiently, 'it's a sport.'

'Oh, is *that* sport?' said Vlad brightening up. 'Oh, if it's about people hitting each other then I like sport. Why do they wear gloves?'

'So they don't do each other too much harm. In the old days they used to box bare fisted and really hurt each other.'

'Ah the good old days!' sighed Vlad nostalgically.

'And then,' went on Paul, 'the Marquis of Queensbury rules were introduced which made it a cleaner game and fewer people got hurt and killed.'

'I don't approve of the Marquis of Queensbury,' complained Vlad, 'and what's more Great Uncle Ghitza wouldn't have either.'

The boxing was followed by rugger.

'What's this game called?' asked Vlad.

'Rugger,' said Paul.

'It's jolly good,' commented Vlad, 'rugger is really great. Brilliant!'

'Skill, skill!' yelled Paul, bouncing on his seat and nearly upsetting the cocoa.

'I like the way they kick each other and get rough,' said Vlad. 'Go on, get him, kick him in the shins, grab him, that's right, well done,' yelled Vlad at the television.

'Vlad, you don't know anything,' snapped Paul. 'The idea of sport isn't that people kick and hurt each other.'

'Isn't it?' said Vlad, sounding disappointed and a bit disbelieving.

After the rugger came soccer. Vlad kept sniffing and yawning and coughing.

'Do be quiet,' said Paul.

'Well I don't like this game,' announced Vlad.

'Football's a great game,' replied Paul indignantly. 'What's wrong with it?'

'Well the only thing they kick in this game is the ball,' complained the vampire.

'Vlad, be quiet,' shouted Paul and Judy together, 'or you won't see the film.'

'Poor old Vlad, poor little Drac,' muttered the vampire and then settled down silently.

The great moment came. There on the screen in large lettering, dripping with blood were the magic words: 'The Curse of the Vampire'.

'Caw,' said Vlad jumping up and down, eyes tight shut. 'It's beginning, it's beginning.'

The film started with a castle in the middle of a black forest; it was a dark and moonless night and the owls shrieked in the blackness. Then out of the forest flew a vampire and settled on the window ledge of a girl's room in an ancient castle. The camera moved in to take a close-up of the vampire's evil face.

'Look! It's Great Uncle Ghitza,' shrieked Vlad. 'Hello Great Uncle Ghitza, it's me, Vlad, your great-nephew – please say hello to me,' begged Vlad.

'Oh Vlad,' said Judy, 'it's not your Great Uncle Ghitza, it's an actor dressed up as a vampire.'

'Are you sure?' asked Vlad.

'Absolutely,' said Judy.

''spose so,' said Vlad. 'But he looked so mean and evil I was sure it was Great Uncle Ghitza. Great Uncle Ghitza doesn't know my name is Vlad does he?'

'No he doesn't,' said Judy. 'Now you settle down and let us all enjoy the film.'

'Yeah, I will,' agreed Vlad. 'I'll be very good and quiet 'cos it's only a film, it's not really real is it?'

'No Vlad,' replied Judy soothingly. 'It's only make believe.'

So Vlad sat watching the film, peering through his fingers and sipping his medicine. During the break for advertisements the children noticed Vlad pacing up and down on the side of the couch frowning.

'What's up Vlad? Aren't you enjoying the film?'

'Got a problem,' muttered the vampire. 'In a dilemma.'

'Do you want to tell us about it?' asked Judy.

Vlad continued to pace. 'Well,' he said. 'It's like being a red Indian watching a Western. I'm a vampire and the vampires are the baddies. I want

to be on the side of the goodies but the goodies are people, so I don't know which side I'm on.'

'Poor Vlad,' said Judy sympathetically.

'It's all well and good for you to say "Poor Vlad",' grumbled the vampire. 'But you're a person and don't have the problem. After all people make all the films, I shall make a horror film in which the vampires are the goodies and the people the baddies. Ummm, Vampire Productions present "The Gentle Vampire" written by Vlad the Drac, produced by Vlad the Drac and starring Vlad the Drac. Yes, that's what I'll do,' and Vlad settled to watch the second half of the film much comforted.

In the second half, however, the vampires started being very vampirish and biting people. Judy and Paul watched fascinated, but Vlad dived behind a cushion muttering:

'I can't watch. Oh dear, he's being so wicked. Look at that – he's vampirising her. I'm sure it's Great Uncle Ghitza. I can't bear to watch,' and he hid behind the cushion.

'Vlad are you scared, shall we turn it off?' asked Judy.

'Oh no,' said Vlad quickly. 'Don't turn it off, just tell me when it's safe for me to look.'

By the time the film came to an end the children were perfectly cheerful and Vlad was shaking behind the cushion.

'That was great wasn't it?' said Paul enthusiastically.

'I really enjoyed it,' agreed Judy. 'Didn't you Vlad?'

'Yes,' said the vampire half-heartedly. 'I suppose so.'

'Look at the time,' said Paul. 'I didn't realize it was so late, we'd better get to bed. We promised to be asleep by the time Mum and Dad came home.'

When their parents came home both children were in bed and apparently sleeping peacefully.

'It can't have been a very frightening film,' said Mr Stone.

'Oh, our children are too sensible to be scared of mythical monsters,' said Mrs Stone cheerfully.

As soon as they had gone Vlad sneaked out of his drawer and climbed into Judy's bed; a few minutes later Judy felt something flapping against her chin.

'Oh Vlad, what are you doing here?'

'Having nightmares,' whimpered the vampire. 'Feel scared.'

'What of?' asked Judy.

'Great Uncle Ghitza might come in the night and vampirise me,' sobbed Vlad.

'Oh Vlad you cuddle up and go to sleep. It was only a film, I'll look after you.'

'I'll try,' whispered Vlad. 'But Judy I don't think I like horror films.'

6

Football Crazy

One Wednesday afternoon, early in December, Paul came home from school early. He went straight upstairs and let Vlad out of his drawer.

'This is a nice surprise,' said Vlad. 'I didn't expect you back for ages.'

'We got sent home early because there was a leak in the classroom ceiling.'

'No Judy?' asked Vlad.

'No, she's still at school.'

'Just us boys together, eh! Jolly good.'

'Ummm well, I'm not too sure about that. We had to bring some school work home with us. I'm going to work on the kitchen table. You can come down to the kitchen with me as everyone is out. But you must play quietly while I do my work.'

Vlad sat on Paul's shoulder as they went downstairs.

'You don't really have to do that boring old school work do you, instead of playing with me?'

'Yes,' said Paul firmly as they reached the kitchen and he put Vlad on the kitchen table. 'Now you just entertain yourself for a little while and don't go near Mum's washing-up liquid. You've got enough of your own.'

'Poor old Vlad, poor little Drac,' complained the vampire. He prowled about looking for something to do until he found a stray pea by the sugar basin. Vlad put the salt pot at one side of the table and the pepper pot at the other and began to play football with the pea. After a few minutes the pea hit the pepper pot and fell on to the floor.

'Goal!' shouted Vlad and ran round the table hugging himself.

'Can I have my pea back?' Vlad asked Paul peering anxiously over the side of the table.

'What?' said Paul, who was deep in thought.

'My football, the pea on the floor,' explained Vlad patiently, 'can I have it back please?'

'Oh sorry Vlad, I've trodden on it,' said Paul apologetically.

'Trust you, with your great big feet,' grumbled Vlad gloomily.

'Just as I was getting a good game going, you go and squash my football.'

'Well I can get you another football – how about a grape?' asked Paul.

'No, too big and squashy,' retorted Vlad.

'Well a peppercorn then?' enquired Paul.

'No too small and hard!' complained Vlad bitterly.

Paul got on with his work until he was rudely interupted by a piercing whistle from Vlad racing round the table.

'Vlad, stop that, it's deafening – what on earth are you doing?'

'I'm umpiring,' replied Vlad huffily. 'Vlad the vampire umpire – what else can I do since you crushed my football?'

'Well not that – it's far too noisy.'

'Not fair. Can't do anything,' complained Vlad. 'Poor old Vlad, poor old Drac. Think I'll apply for a transfer.'

'No one else would have you,' said Paul crushingly.

'Wish I was back under my stone,' muttered Vlad and leapt up to a shelf.

Paul went back to his work while Vlad grumbled to himself.

When Judy came home she asked:

'Where's Vlad?'

'Oh he's sulking somewhere.'

'Poor Vlad, what's he sulking about?'

'He squashed my football,' shouted Vlad from his shelf.

'Oh Vlad, there you are. However did you get up there?'

'I flew,' said Vlad.

'I didn't know you could fly Vlad.'

'Neither did I,' said the vampire in a surprised tone. 'I don't know how I did it – aren't I clever? If I learned to fly I might learn to vampirise.'

'Oh no, Vlad, don't do that. But I think you're very clever to fly. Are you going to fly down now?'

Vlad stood on the edge of the shelf and spread his cloak, then he staggered back.

'What's wrong Vlad?'

'Dizzy, when I look down,' said Vlad. 'Feel scared, you'll have to come and get me.'

Judy was just climbing on to a chair to get Vlad when they heard the front door bang.

'Quick Vlad, hide,' whispered Judy. So Vlad scuttled along the shelf. Jars and pots rattled and shook until he climbed into a plant pot and covered himself with foliage.

A second later Mr Stone came in carrying a block of ice-cream.

'Hello you two,' he said putting down his violin case. 'I'll just get some dishes and we can share out this ice-cream before it melts.'

'I'll get them,' said Paul and Judy together, trying to divert him from the shelves.

While they were eating the ice-cream, Mr Stone said:

'I've got two tickets for the soccer international on Saturday, Paul. Someone in the orchestra gave them to me.'

Something behind the plant rustled and Judy sneaked a look at Vlad's face peering out between the branches, his eyes shining with interest.

'That sounds great, Dad,' said Paul enthusiastically, 'I'd love to go.'

'Can't I come?' said Judy.

''course not,' said Paul. 'Girls don't like football.'

'I do,' said Judy. 'I watch it on TV when you do, so why shouldn't I go to a live match as well?'

'Sorry Judy,' said Dad, 'but I've only got two

tickets, next time I'll take you. Now I'm off to practise for a while.'

As soon as Mr Stone had gone, Vlad appeared from behind the plant. 'Get me down from here quick, Judy. I've got to have a chat with my friend Paul.'

'Your friend?' said Paul. 'I thought we weren't talking.'

''course we're talking old pal,' said Vlad genially, as Judy lifted him down from the shelf. Vlad went and sat on Paul's shoulder and gently nibbled his ear.

'What's all this for Vlad?' asked Paul suspiciously.

'You will take me to the football match, won't you?' Vlad cajoled. Seeing as how I was so good while you were doing your homework.'

'You were anything but good,' Paul remonstrated.

'Well, I would have been if I'd known you were going to a football match.'

Judy laughed at Vlad's honesty. 'Oh, Paul you'd better take him, he's obviously dying to go.'

'Caw, yes,' said Vlad. 'Can I have a scarf and a rattle and shout like they do on television?'

'No,' said Paul emphatically. 'If you do come you will have to be very quiet.'

'Oh, I will be,' agreed Vlad. 'I'll sit on your shoulder and peep out over the tip of your sweater and be as quiet as a mouse.'

'Okay, it's a bargain. If you are good until Saturday, I'll take you,' said Paul reluctantly.

For three days Vlad struggled to be good and his efforts were rewarded.

'Something tells me I'm making a mistake,' said Paul as Judy tried to persuade the excited young vampire to stay still and stop practising rattle noises.

'It's all right for some. I'll have to stay in and kick my heels while you lucky creatures are having a whale of a time.'

Late on Saturday afternoon Mr Stone and Paul returned from the match. When she heard the sound of a key in the lock, Judy ran to the top of the stairs. But when she saw them she stopped.

Dad, grim faced, was shutting the door, he had a black eye and a torn collar, he was holding Paul's arm and Paul looked white and bedraggled, with his hair dishevelled and his jacket torn.

'Whatever happened to you two?' asked Mrs Stone in amazement, as she came through into the hall.

'Your son,' said Dad in a furious voice, 'behaved in the most appalling way. I was really ashamed of him. I can't imagine where he learnt the language he was using. He behaved like a professional football hooligan – it's lucky we weren't arrested.'

'Oh Paul,' said Mrs Stone, 'that doesn't sound like you. What happened?'

Paul just scowled and muttered something unintelligible.

'You just go upstairs to your room and stay there,' said Dad. 'You can eat up there, I'm thoroughly ashamed of you.'

Paul stormed up the stairs. As he passed Judy he yanked Vlad from his pocket and thrust him into Judy's hand.

'Here, you have him – I never want to set eyes on the horrible little monster again.'

Paul walked into his room and slammed the door. Judy darted into her room and set Vlad down on the bed.

'Oh, Vlad, what have you been up to? What have you done this time?'

'Was very bad,' whispered the crestfallen vampire.

'Were you really?' said Judy.

Vlad nodded miserably. 'Got over excited,' he informed Judy. 'Do you think Paul will ever forgive me – he's very angry.'

'I think you ought to apologize for whatever it was you did, don't you Vlad?'

The vampire nodded again.

'Feel scared, Judy. Don't think Paul likes me anymore.'

'Were you that bad?'

'Yes, I was very bad – I don't know what came over me – just got 'cited you see.'

'Come on, let's go and apologize to Paul.'

Judy took Vlad and knocked on Paul's door.

'Paul, Vlad wants to apologize.'

'I'm not interested,' snapped Paul.

Judy opened the door and went in.

'Please Paul – just listen to what Vlad has to say.'

Paul was lying on his bed, face down, he turned his face to the wall when they came in.

Vlad went and stood right near Paul's ear and whispered:

'Sorry I was bad Paul and got over-excited and got you into trouble. If you tell me what I can do to make it up to you I will.'

Paul took no notice.

'Really am very sorry,' Vlad went on, tears rolling down his face. 'Didn't mean to be bad.'

Paul still took no notice. Vlad began to cry.

'You see Judy, Paul doesn't like me anymore.'

'Oh, Paul, Vlad's so miserable, please talk to him. It can't have been that bad.'

'Jolly well was,' said Paul indignantly. 'Ask him what happened.'

'What happened Vlad?' asked Judy. 'I'm dying to know.'

'Go on, you tell her how awful you were,' said Paul.

'All right,' said Vlad in a small voice. He looked at his feet. 'Well,' he began, 'it was all right during the match. I just watched and yelled like everyone else and no one took any notice. Then when it was over the crowd tried to run on to the pitch, and the police came to stop us, and then I got over 'cited and shouted "Knock his helmet off, knock the copper's helmet off".'

'You said that?' gasped Judy.

Vlad nodded.

'Yes, he certainly did,' said Paul 'At the top of his voice, and Dad assumed it was me and was furious.'

'Oh, dear,' said Judy, 'what happened next?'

'Some Scotsman did knock the policeman's helmet off,' said Paul grimly, 'and Vlad had something to say to them.'

'Whatever did you say to the Scotsman?' asked Judy.

Vlad looked even more miserable. 'Can't remember,' he muttered.

'Oh, yes you can,' said Paul.

'I asked them if it was draughty up their kilts,'

confessed Vlad.

Judy giggled. 'Oh, Vlad you didn't.'

'I did,' Vlad assured her, 'and then one of the Scotsmen went to hit Paul and your Dad stopped him and got a black eye.'

'That was very naughty Vlad,' said Judy trying hard not to laugh. 'Then what?'

'Then I went mad,' said Vlad, beginning to giggle too. 'I yelled "Manchester United" and then "Up the Arsenal" and then "Chelsea for ever".'

'He really did,' said Paul. 'And within two minutes everyone was fighting everyone. You've never seen anything like it.'

Judy laughed. 'That little thing got all those people fighting?'

Paul began to laugh too. 'It was rather funny, now I come to think of it,' he said.

'What happened next?'

'Well,' said Vlad, who was beginning to cheer up, 'it was a big mess and I went on yelling (I didn't know I knew that many teams), until lots of policemen came up,' Vlad wiped his eyes, 'and then they were going to arrest Dad and Paul, so Dad said "so sorry officer, I just don't know what got into my son, he's never behaved like this before, I guarantee it won't happen again".' At this point Vlad was laughing so much he fell off the bed.

Judy picked him up.

'Hurt my head,' said Vlad rubbing his head and beginning to giggle again.

'Serve you right,' said both the children together, but all three of them went on laughing.

'Shake hands Paul?' asked Vlad.

'Well, all right,' said Paul, 'but I'll never take you anywhere again no matter how many "Poor little Vlads, poor old Dracs" you come out with.'

'Poor old Vlad, poor little Drac,' corrected Vlad.

'Does it make any difference?' asked Paul.

'Well,' answered Vlad. 'I'm *not* little Vlad, just a little vampire. I think you should get it right, that's all.'

'One day, I'll get you right,' threatened Paul.

7
Christmas

It was a week before Christmas and Judy was wrapping presents. Vlad inspected each of them until he found a tiny one which said, 'To Vlad, Happy Christmas and New Year, Love Judy and Paul'.

'Caw,' said Vlad. 'This one's for me, can I open it now?'

'No,' said Judy taking it away. 'You have got to wait till December 25th.'

'Can't wait that long,' said Vlad looking miserable. 'I've never had a present, not never in my whole life and now you're making me wait even longer – it's not fair.'

'Don't be silly Vlad, thinking about it beforehand is half the fun.'

'Speak for yourself,' grumbled the vampire. 'Want my present now.'

'Well you can't have it and that's that,' said Judy firmly.

'Poor old Vlad . . . ,' muttered Vlad.

'Poor little Drac,' joined in Judy. 'You can't pull that one anymore.'

Vlad gave up and went and stood on the window-sill, wrapped his cloak round his head and began to move along making a strange noise.

'Vlad, whatever are you doing?' asked Judy.

'My vampire dance,' said Vlad. 'I watched "Come Dancing" on television and I've made up a vampire dance.'

'Oh, is that what it was. You know Vlad, you're actually quite scary when you do that.'

Vlad let his cloak drop.

'Who's scary? Me? Caw, am I really? Like Great Uncle Ghitza?' And Vlad rushed over to the mirror and did his vampire dance peeping at himself from under his left arm. He staggered back to Judy white and shaking, 'I scared me,' he told her.

'Poor little Vlad,' laughed Judy. 'But you're not as small as you used to be. You know you're definitely getting bigger.'

'I know,' said Vlad proudly puffing out his chest, 'it's that super strength washing-up liquid you've been getting me. It's making me big and strong. I'd like to be big, but I hope it doesn't make me like other vampires. I don't want to get a taste for blood. And I don't want to be so big that you can't take me to places.'

Paul came into the room.

'Look at Vlad, Paul,' said Judy. 'He can do a really scary vampire dance.'

'Let's see Vlad,' said Paul.

'All right,' agreed the vampire, but he kept well away from the mirror for the demonstration.

'That's very good Vlad, you quite alarmed me.

Hey Judy, Mum says we can have a fancy dress party on Christmas Eve.'

'What's a fancy dress party?' asked Vlad. 'Is it something nice?'

'Yes,' said Paul enthusiastically. 'You have to dress up. All our friends will come here and we'll play games and have nice things to eat.'

'Sounds good,' said Vlad. 'Can I come?'

'No, of course not – you know you have to be a secret, if you want to stay here with us and not end up in a museum or a zoo.'

'It's not fair,' complained Vlad. 'I never meet anyone 'cept you and Judy. You have lots of people to talk to but I don't – it's almost as bad as being under my stone. Poor old Vlad . . .'

'Poor little Drac,' chorused both the children.

'Now Vlad, be reasonable,' said Judy who could see that the vampire was nearly in tears. 'It's all for your own good, you must understand that.'

'Sometimes think I'd rather be in a museum or a zoo,' sniffed Vlad. 'Get very lonely. Please, please let me come to your party. I'll be very good and you can tell your friends that I'm very nice if they're quiet about me, but if they tell anyone I'll do my scary vampire dance and then I'll come and vampirise them in the night.'

'Don't like that idea one bit,' said Paul. 'Anyway Vlad, this is a fancy dress party.'

'What's fancy dress?'

'Dressing up as something you're not, like a pirate or a gypsy or a tin of soup or William

Shakespeare or something.'

'I could go as Great Uncle Ghitza,' suggested Vlad brightly.

'No,' yelled both children.

'All right, all right,' said Vlad. 'Have to think of something else – I know what, I saw something in a history book in the Roman section.'

'Whatever do you mean?' asked Judy.

'Show you,' said Vlad, and he went through the book until he came to a picture of a gladiator with a sword, a shield and a net. 'One of those.'

'Oh, a gladiator,' said Judy, 'they used to fight each other while the crowds watched.'

'Well, I'll go as one of those. Vlad the Glad, most famous of all the gladiators,' gurgled the vampire, delighted with his pun.

'The trouble is, he probably will find a way of smuggling himself to the party,' said Paul.

And he did, carrying a two-pronged fork, holding the lid of the egg poacher and wearing a hair net. Vlad was a great success with the other children. He sang his vampire song and danced his vampire dance and the children thoroughly enjoyed being scared by his vampire act.

'Do it again Vlad,' they shouted as Vlad clacked his teeth and flicked tomato juice at the children.

'All right,' said Vlad. 'But you must promise not to tell anyone about me or I'll have to go to a museum or a zoo and you wouldn't want that would you?'

Fortunately, the children didn't believe Vlad

was real. They thought he was a clever electronic doll. But all the same they promised Judy and Paul that they wouldn't say a word about him.

As the children left Vlad gave them each a balloon. He took a little sail up in the air with the last balloon just for fun, and then went and stood on the window-sill and waved them goodbye.

'That was nice,' said Vlad cheerfully. 'I liked your friends and they thought I was wonderful. I really should become a film star. I could be a children's vampire and star in horror films that are only slightly frightening. Could you arrange for me to have an audition?'

'Don't get ideas, Vlad. They didn't even believe you were a vampire. They all think you are a doll we brought back from our holidays. And if they thought for a moment that you were a real bloodsucking vampire, they'd soon split on you. They'd be down to the police station as fast as their legs could carry them.'

'I'd vampirise them, if they did,' scowled Vlad.

'You couldn't vampirise a sausage,' said Paul taking the last one from the plate.

'I know, I know,' agreed Vlad gloomily. 'My Great Uncle Ghitza wouldn't be very proud of me, would he?'

The children tidied up after the party and then went to look for Vlad. He was nowhere to be seen.

'I hope he hasn't run away to be a film star,' said Judy in a worried tone. 'We'd better check the sitting-room.'

They went into the sitting-room. At the far end was the tree, twinkling with lights, coloured balls and strands of tinsel. All round it were presents in beautiful wrapping paper and coloured ribbons. But Vlad was nowhere to be seen.

'He's nowhere here,' said Paul. 'I hope he hasn't been tampering with these parcels.'

'Coo eee,' said Vlad's voice.

'He's here somewhere,' said Judy and then her eye caught sight of the fairy from the Christmas tree lying on the floor. The doll had two tooth marks on its neck. And there at the top of the tree, in the fairy's place, was Vlad balancing on one foot, holding up his gladiator's fork like a wand.

'Look, Paul, there he is pretending to be the fairy on the Christmas tree. And look what he's done to the real fairy.'

'Oh, no,' exploded Paul. 'Vlad, the fairy on the Christmas tree is supposed to be pretty. You can't want to be pretty and frightening at the same time, Vlad.'

'Oh, yes I can,' retorted the vampire. 'I can want to. It's managing it that's the problem.'

'Well you just come down and explain how the fairy got those marks on her neck.'

'All right,' grumbled Vlad. 'Poor old Vlad . . .'

'Poor little fairy. Not poor little Drac,' said Judy.

'I only kissed her,' said Vlad. 'She tastes like soap. I rather like her. Wish she was real. She'd be my friend. Not like you. She'd be nice to me. She'd give me my present,' sulked the vampire.

'You are so spoilt, Vlad, you don't deserve a present,' said Judy holding the chair while Paul stretched up to replace the wounded fairy.

'What would you like for your present, anyway?' relented Judy as she saw tears welling into Vlad's eyes.

'I'd like a lady vampire,' said Vlad without hesitation.

Paul and Judy looked at each other, trying not to giggle.

'Oh, dear,' said Judy, 'that's going to be a problem, Vlad.'

'I know,' said the vampire wistfully. 'I mean I'm only a little vampire now. But when I grow up what will I do?'

'I've never thought of you growing up,' said Judy 'But you are, of course.'

'When we first met you,' said Paul, 'you said you thought you might be the last of the vampires.'

'I know,' wept Vlad. 'I might never meet a lady vampire. I'll never have a friend like myself.' And he curled up in a wailing heap of self pity.

Judy picked him up and kissed him.

'Don't worry Vlad, we'll think of something when the time comes. Meanwhile, lets have a lovely Christmas.'

On Christmas Day the children opened their stockings. Vlad was delighted with his tin of polish and a book on 'The Dracula Legend'. 'I'll read it before I go to sleep,' he told Judy.

'No you won't,' Judy told him, 'you'll have

71

nightmares and keep me awake. We'll read it together in the daylight.'

When the children went downstairs they found their parents holding a basket that barked.

'What's that?' asked Paul.

'You kept complaining that you wanted a pet. So here you are,' said Mrs Stone.

'A puppy!' said Judy, wondering what Vlad would say.

'A puppy,' said Paul delightedly. 'Let's have a look.'

They opened the basket and in it was a scruffy little dog with long silky ears.

'Aah, he's lovely,' said Paul, lifting the puppy out of the box. 'What shall we call him Judy?'

'I don't know,' said Judy, trying to imagine how the vampire would cope with the spaniel, and vice versa.

'Don't you like the puppy, Judy?' asked Mrs Stone.

'Yes he's lovely,' said Judy as the dog licked her fingers and rubbed his head against her.

That evening Judy took Vlad a Christmas drink of floor polish which he gulped down.

'I don't like Christmas,' complained the vampire. 'I'm left all on my own all day, it's worse than other days. Please Judy, let me come down and I'll sit somewhere where I can't be seen and just look at what's going on.'

'Well Vlad, there's a complication,' confessed Judy. 'Mum and Dad gave Paul and me a dog for Christmas and it's with us downstairs.'

'A dog!' said Vlad in a disgusted tone. Then he began to tremble and climbed into the bottom of the drawer under all Judy's scarves and socks.

'Close the drawer,' he yelled.

'But Vlad,' reasoned Judy, 'the dog won't do you any harm, why don't you just try making friends with him?'

'Never,' said Vlad. 'Shall just live alone and die alone in this drawer. It's not much worse than being under a stone. I'll be all right. Don't worry about me. You go back to all your family and your presents and your pet. I don't need you. Off you go, I feel like going to sleep.'

'Oh, Vlad, I'm sure if you just met the dog you'd feel different, he's so sweet.'

'I'm sure he's delightful Judy, I'd just rather keep myself to myself. Goodnight, now please be so kind as to shut my drawer. Thank you.'

For days everyone had a peaceful time while Vlad sulked in his drawer, refusing to come out or talk to Judy or Paul. Then the children's grandmother and aunt came to stay. One afternoon Gran was having a rest when there was a shriek from her room. Mrs Stone and the children rushed up.

'Something bit my ankle – look,' said Gran clasping her foot.

'Oh dear,' said Mrs Stone as she put some

disinfectant on the wound. 'It must be the new puppy. It seemed like such a sweet little thing.'

'It's odd,' said Gran, 'I didn't see the dog either before or after the bite. Still it must have been the dog. Maybe I kicked him by accident and didn't realize.'

The very next day when Aunt Margot was watching television, *she* suddenly shrieked and clasped her ankle. Dad rushed over and looked.

'She's been bitten just like gran. That dog must be vicious.'

'I didn't see the dog anywhere near,' said Mrs Stone. 'I thought he was in his basket in the kitchen.'

'So did I,' said Paul.

'Well, he can't have been,' said Judy, surreptitiously kicking Paul.

'It's odd,' said Dad, 'but those teeth marks don't look like a dog bite.'

'Maybe we've got mice,' suggested Judy.

'Or a rat,' said Paul under his breath.

'Stop talking nonsense, Paul,' said Mr Stone. 'There are no rats in this house. We'll have to take that dog back to the pet shop, he's obviously too dangerous to stay here, get your coat and we'll take him straight away. I'll go and get him. Don't you touch him.'

While they were gone, Judy went up to Vlad's drawer.

'Vlad!'

She was greeted by the sound of loud snoring.

76

'Vlad, it's no good pretending, I know you're awake, Dad and Paul are taking that poor little puppy back to the pet shop.'

'Oh really,' said Vlad in a bored tone, yawning and stretching.

'Vlad stop pretending. I know it was you that bit Gran and Aunt Margot. Paul is going to be absolutely furious with you.'

'All right, I confess, but you see Judy I had to do it, I just had to get rid of that dog or he would have eaten me.'

'Nonsense, Vlad.'

'Yes, he would,' insisted the vampire. 'He was so big. I didn't enjoy biting them you know. I feel quite sick, from the taste, but it was self-defence. You can't have vampires and dogs in the same house. It was me or him and there is nowhere else for me to go. Poor old Vlad, poor little Drac, no one loves me, not no one in the whole world.'

'I love you Vlad,' said Judy, feeling very sorry for the vampire. Vlad buried his head in Judy's hair.

'You'll explain to Paul, won't you, why poor old Vlad had to look after himself?'

'I'll try Vlad,' promised Judy. 'But it won't be easy.'

'I have faith in you Judy,' stated Vlad confidently. 'Then Paul will love me again too and it will be just as if nothing ever happened.'

8

Vlad gets Airborne

'Look what I found in Paul's room,' announced Vlad and banged down a tin, ' "Anti-V Powder".'

'Well,' said Judy, 'what about it?'

'What I want to know is what does that V stand for?'

'Vermin, mice and things like that, nasty things you want to get rid of.'

'I see,' said Vlad suspiciously, ' 'spect Paul thinks I'm vermin. 'Spect he does. 'Spect he thinks I'm vermin. Or else it's specially for me, anti-vampire powder or anti-Vlad powder.'

'Oh Vlad, that's silly.'

'No it's not, Paul doesn't like me. He's always blaming me for things, even when it's not my fault. And it's not just me personally, he doesn't like vampires, he's prejudiced against us. I couldn't help being born a vampire.'

'Vlad, Paul does like you. But you keep getting him into trouble.'

'Don't,' muttered Vlad. 'Anyway I don't care. I've started my own party.' And Vlad showed Judy a badge with A-P on it.

'What on earth does A-P stand for Vlad?' asked Judy. 'I hope it's not Anti-Paul.'

'Not sure,' grumbled Vlad. 'Haven't decided if it's anti-people or just anti-Paul.'

'But Vlad if you start being anti-people you'll have to be anti-me too.'

'Well you're different – I could make you an honorary vampire or something.'

'But I don't want to be a vampire when I'm a person, and Vlad you can't be anti-people, you'd be so outnumbered, the odds are so against you.'

'If I started behaving like Great Uncle Ghitza they would even up a bit! People had better watch out, I've tried to be good and nice and what good has it done me? Now I'm so big I'm going to be a real vampire. I'm going to write a book. If a vampire wrote the truth about vampires, people would sit up and take notice.'

'Yes, Vlad, I expect they would,' said Judy sadly.

'They jolly well would,' insisted Vlad, 'very different. Great Uncle Ghitza would be a big hero and be called Ghitza the Liberator and I'd say you were the only nice person. I'll call my book "Of Vampires and Men" or "A History of the Vampire Speaking People".'

'Oh dear Vlad, what can I do to cheer you up?'

'Nothing,' said Vlad. 'I'll never be happy again. I'll just sit alone in my drawer and write my great book explaining vampires to people and people to vampires.'

'Oh, I see,' said Judy. 'That's a pity because I was thinking you might like to come with me, when I go to the air show with Mum and Dad and Paul.'

'No,' said Vlad. 'I'll stay at home in my drawer, it's better that way, I only get into trouble when I go out – you go and enjoy yourself. I don't mind being alone anymore, I've got used to it,' and Vlad climbed back into his drawer. A moment or two later his head popped out: 'What's an air show?'

'Why do you want to know Vlad, since you don't want to come?'

'Just curious,' replied Vlad.

'Well it's aeroplanes flying round together, making patterns in the sky and turning over and doing clever things.'

'Aeroplanes,' said Vlad brightening up. 'Like we came back from Romania in? Those big vampiry things?'

'That's right,' said Judy.

'Caw,' said Vlad, 'why didn't you say so?'

'But you said you didn't want to go anywhere,' said Judy indignantly.

'You've talked me into it,' replied Vlad cheerfully. 'But if I'm to go out in the sun, I need a hat.'

'Try this bottle top,' said Judy unscrewing her handcream and plonking the cap on Vlad's head. 'Oh, it looks like a helmet.'

'Take it off,' came a muffled reply, 'I can't see, I can't breathe, there's slime all over me.'

Judy removed it laughing. 'Sorry Vlad, but you did look funny.'

'Did I indeed,' said Vlad. 'I'll thank you not to make fun of me. Can't you think of a proper hat for me, a summer hat?'

'What you need is a straw boater,' decided Judy.

'What's that?' asked Vlad.

So Judy showed him a picture of a boy wearing a boater. 'It's a flat straw hat,' she explained.

'Oh yes, I'd look good in one of those,' said Vlad eagerly.

So Judy made him one out of an old straw shopping bag and Vlad tried it on and rushed to the mirror to admire himself.

'Does it look nice?' he asked anxiously.

'Yes, you look wonderful Vlad,' Judy assured him.

At that moment Paul came in and looked at Vlad in amazement.

'Good God, Vlad, you look even more horrible than usual: What is that awful thing you're wearing on your head?

Where did you get that hat,
Where did you get that hat?'

'It's my boater,' said the vampire in a small voice.

'A vampire in a boater,' laughed Paul. 'That's the silliest thing I ever heard – you look ridiculous,' and he collapsed with laughter.

Vlad took the boater off and gave it back to Judy.

'Thanks for making me a boater Judy but I

think I'll stay in my drawer and write my book,' and tearfully Vlad climbed into the drawer.

'Can I have my drawer shut, please,' he asked politely.

Judy shut the drawer.

'Paul, why are you being so nasty to Vlad? I'd just cheered him up and now you've upset him again.'

'Well he did look jolly silly in that hat. And what's more I liked that puppy. I've always wanted a dog. It was your fault, he had to go Judy. You spoilt that awful little soap sucker. I'd rather have a dog.'

'You are being horrid. Vlad was very frightened of the puppy. He may have seemed small and sweet to us but I expect he looked like a lion to Vlad.'

'I suppose so,' sighed Paul. 'But I wish we'd left him under his stone.'

'Ssh, he'll hear you,' said Judy. 'It's bad enough already. Vlad found some anti-V powder in your room and convinced himself it's anti-Vlad powder.'

'Oh, dear,' groaned Paul. 'I'd better try and make it up with him, or we'll have worse havoc.' And he went and knocked on Vlad's drawer.

'Go away,' yelled Vlad. 'I'm out.'

'Vlad, can I open this drawer and have a talk with you?' asked Paul politely.

'No,' shouted Vlad, 'I don't like you – you're anti-vampire, you're not my friend any more, you're always picking on me and laughing at me.'

'I'm very sorry Vlad, I have been nasty and if you open your drawer I'll give you a present.'

There was a moment's silence, then Vlad said:

'All right I agree to talk but we're not friends, yet.'

'All right Vlad, I'll just go and get the present,' said Paul.

A moment later he re-appeared with the helmet from an action-man soldier. 'Here you are Vlad, here's your present. I'm sorry I laughed at your boater.'

Vlad looked at the helmet and his eyes lit up.

'Caw, a real helmet. Just like soldiers wear.' Vlad tried it on.

'How does it look?' he asked Paul nervously.

'Fantastic,' said Paul.

'Incredible,' said Judy.

'After a lot of consideration I have decided to accept your peace-offering Paul,' said Vlad seriously, and he held out his hand.

Equally seriously Paul took it and they shook hands.

'Vlad's coming with us to the air show on Saturday,' said Judy.

'Yes, I am,' agreed Vlad. 'And that's why I need a hat.'

'Oh, no,' groaned Paul. 'Look what happened last time we took you out.'

'I won't do it again, I promise,' said Vlad quickly.

'You promised to be good at the footall match and remember what you did?'

'You won't let me forget, will you, you keep on and on? That was the last time I went out. I've been stuck in for months without complaining . . .'

'Without complaining!' said the children together.

'Well, I did say a little something now and again,' admitted Vlad and he took off his hat to admire it and dropped it on his foot.

'Ouch, ohh, ahh,' he shouted, hopping around holding his toe.

'For goodness sake Vlad, stop making all that noise, it can't be that bad,' said Paul unsympathetically.

'How would you know, it's not your toe,' retorted Vlad indignantly and went on nursing his toe tenderly and yelling intermittently.

'Vlad, do stop,' said Judy, 'someone will hear.'

'Are you two all right up there?' came Dad's voice.

'Yes Dad!' called back Paul. 'I just stubbed my toe that's all.'

'Oh,' said Mr Stone, 'I thought at least five people were being murdered.'

'You thought fast, ' said Vlad approvingly to Paul.

'Yes and I'm getting a bit sick of lying to cover up for you.'

'Can I still come to the air show?' asked Vlad.

'Paul, we've just got to take him with us, he

84

hasn't been out for ages.'

'All right,' said Paul. 'But I wash my hands of the whole business – you take all the responsibility.'

'I will,' said Judy.

'I won't let you down,' Vlad assured her. And he didn't.

He sat all day under Judy's anorak, peeping out at the aeroplanes, wearing his helmet for protection. He followed the planes as they flew in and dived and turned in mid-air.

'Caw,' he said a couple of times. 'Even Great Uncle Ghitza couldn't do that. Caw!'

There was a team called the Red Arrows performing. Vlad watched wide-eyed as they flew in formations constantly changing patterns and groupings.

'Caw,' he muttered. 'They're ever so good, I doubt if even a team of vampires could do that.'

All the way back in the car Vlad slept quietly. Mr and Mrs Stone didn't even suspect that they had an extra passenger.

'That went well, didn't it Paul?' said Judy triumphantly as she put the sleeping vampire in to his drawer.

'It did,' agreed Paul. 'He must be growing up, he was no trouble at all.'

But the next Monday after school, when Judy and Paul turned into their road they heard the oddest noises.

'Whatever's that?' said Paul.

'I don't know,' replied Judy nervously, 'but it seems to be coming from our house.'

As they raced along the street a neighbour came out.

'There's the oddest noises coming from your house,' said Mrs Woodstock. 'I've knocked at the door, but I can't get anyone to answer.'

'It must be Dad – he's composing music for a war film – that's what it must be.'

'Well I suppose that's it,' agreed Mrs Woodstock. 'I expect he didn't hear when I rang.'

'I'm not surprised,' said Judy as the bangings and crashings and tinklings started again.

'I was just thinking of calling the police,' said Mrs Woodstock.

'I'm glad you didn't,' said Paul. 'We'd better go and tell Dad that he's deafening the whole street and then he'll stop.'

The children raced home and dashed into the music room to see Vlad standing at one end of the piano keys, 'Look at me,' he yelled, delighted to have an audience. 'One, two, three, go,' and Vlad raced down the piano keys and took off from the end of the piano, and began to turn and twist in the air, making an unearthly whirring sound.

'Whatever do you think you're doing?' yelled Paul.

Vlad was a bit out of breath, 'I'm an aerobatic vampire,' he panted.

'Whatever were you doing with the piano?'

'It's my musical runway,' explained Vlad

proudly. 'Music while I work.'

'But Vlad,' said Judy, 'the noise was terrible, the neighbours were just going to call the police.'

'Oh dear,' said Vlad miserably. 'I was having such a good time, I didn't even think of that. Sorry Judy I didn't mean to be bad.'

'Well, no harm done this time Vlad, but you must be more careful.'

'I will, I promise,' agreed Vlad. 'Sorry Paul.

'Vlad you absolutely must stay in your own room. You must stop wandering all round the house.'

'Where can I practise my aerobatics?' asked Vlad anxiously. 'What can I use as a runway?'

'I suppose it's all right if you close the piano and make sure everyone is out,' said Judy.

Vlad practised on the closed piano. 'It's not as much fun,' he said sadly. 'But I 'spose it's safer and I won't end up in a museum or a zoo. Still everything goes wrong for me . . .'

'Poor old Vlad, poor little Drac,' chorused Judy and Paul.

'You took the words right out of my mouth,' agreed Vlad.

9
Vlad Discovered

'Paul,' said Judy one morning, 'I've decided to take Vlad to school.'

'Do you really think that's a good idea Judy?' asked Paul. 'I know he's been much better lately, but I do think you're asking for trouble.'

'But Paul, poor little Vlad hardly ever goes out and he's lonely. I promised I'd take him if he was good for a month and since that incident with the piano he's been very nice and quiet and he does so much want to go to school just once.'

'Well on your head be it,' said Paul. 'I wouldn't risk it myself.'

But Judy put Vlad in the pocket of her dress and took him off to school. He sat happily looking around, while Miss Fairfax took the register and remained silent all through prayers. In fact all went so well that Judy nearly forgot that Vlad was there. Judy got out her project book on vampires and began to work on it.

'Are you *still* working on the vampire book?' said Miss Fairfax's voice.

'Yes Miss Fairfax,' replied Judy. 'I'm very interested in vampires.'

'Really Judy this has been going on for too long.

It's nearly a year since you went to Romania and you've been writing about vampires ever since. I really think it's time you started a project on something more sensible and worthwhile. Vampires do not and never have existed. They are entirely mythical creatures and are not worth worrying about or writing about.'

This was too much for Vlad. He flew out of Judy's pocket and stood on her desk jumping up and down with rage.

'Madam,' he began to the amazed Miss Fairfax. 'How dare you suggest that vampires don't exist. They most certainly do exist. I myself am a vampire, Vlad the Drac by name and what's more I come from a long line of vampires and you have offended my father and my father's father and my father's father's father before him. You can be jolly glad I'm not my Great Uncle Ghitza or I'd vampirise you on the spot.'

Miss Fairfax looked at the furious little vampire in horrified amazement.

Vlad spread his cloak over his head and paced up and down Judy's desk muttering to himself:

'Not exist indeed, what a cheek! Some people! No such things as vampires, what ignorance!'

Miss Fairfax turned as white as a sheet and then fainted.

Vlad heard the crash as she fell and peeped out from under his cloak. 'She fainted,' he said in an amazed tone to Judy. 'Did you see that? I vampirised her. Who would ever have believed it

possible. Oh children, children, this is the happiest day of my life, I vampirised someone. I'm a real vampire at last. If only Great Uncle Ghitza was here to see me in my moment of glory.'

One little girl began to cry. Vlad flew over to her.

'Don't be scared,' he told her re-assuringly. 'It's only old Vlad having himself a bit of fun. Nothing to be frightened of. Is that red paint you've got there? You don't mind if I borrow that brush for a moment do you?'

'It's all up now. Oh dear, whatever is going to happen?' wailed Judy.

Later that evening Paul and Judy and Vlad sat in a line on Judy's bed waiting for the inevitable phone call.

'I had to do it,' explained Vlad. 'She offended vampires, if I hadn't vampirised her Great Uncle Ghitza would never have forgiven me.'

'What's the difference now?' groaned Paul. 'As soon as Mum and Dad get to hear about it you'll go to the zoo or a museum anyway.'

'Don't care,' retorted Vlad. 'The honour of the vampires has been defended.'

Then the phone rang. Paul opened the bedroom door so that they could all hear the conversation.

'Don't be absurd,' said Mr Stone, 'that's the silliest statement I've ever heard. Of course my children don't have a pet vampire – how can you bring yourself to phone me up and ask such a crazy question. I'm afraid I'm not prepared to discuss the matter one moment longer. Good evening,' and down went the phone.

'I think he sounds a bit cross,' commented Vlad.

'Paul, Judy, will you please come down,' called Mr Stone.

'Here we go,' said Paul, 'C-o-m-i-n-g.'

'Children,' said Mrs Stone, 'Dad's just had the strangest phone-call from your headmaster. He says something crazy about you having a pet vampire.'

'Yes,' said Paul. 'Well, it's true we have.'

'Good God,' said Mr Stone, 'is this some kind of practical joke?'

'No Dad,' said Judy. 'It's true.'

'It can't be true,' said Mrs Stone. 'Everyone knows they don't exist.'

'Oh, yes they do,' yelled a small angry voice from above.

'Good lord,' said Mr Stone. 'I can't believe it.'

'Come down Vlad. Mum and Dad want to meet you,' said Paul.

' 'Course they do,' said Vlad, 'Don't worry about a thing, leave it all to me.'

The little vampire smartened himself up and slid down the banister to the hall.

'Dad, this is Vlad the Drac, our pet vampire.'

'How do you do Sir,' said Vlad holding out his hand.

'How do you do,' said Mr Stone looking a bit dazed as he shook Vlad's hand.

'It's a pleasure to meet you at last,' said Vlad.

'I've been wanting to thank you for the hospitality I've enjoyed in your house for so long and to say how much I've enjoyed your afternoon performance on the violin.'

'Not at all,' muttered Mr Stone. 'It's a pleasure. Just how long have you been here?'

'Nearly a year,' said Vlad. 'I came back with you from Romania.'

'Good gracious,' said Mr Stone.

'You don't have to worry,' Vlad re-assured him. 'I'm quite harmless, I'm a vegetarian.'

'Vlad, I think you should meet Mum now,' said Judy.

Vlad turned to look at Mrs Stone and then burst into tears.

'Forgive me,' he sobbed. 'But you remind me of my own dear mother, who's been dead for nearly a hundred years.'

'Oh,' said Mrs Stone, who was not sure whether she was flattered or not, 'you poor little thing, come and sit on my knee.'

So Vlad dried his eyes, winked at Judy and Paul and went and sat on their mother's knee and told her all about the ravine and Great Uncle Ghitza and why he'd had to vampirise Miss Fairfax. Mrs Stone listened fascinated, then she remembered she was hostess.

'Can I offer you something to eat?' she said politely. 'A saucer of milk perhaps?'

'Oh no,' said Vlad. 'I hate milk! I only like soap and washing-up liquid, and shoe polish and—'

'Washing-up liquid! I wondered why I never seem to have any.'

'That's right,' said Vlad. 'I can't bear to see you washing up with my supper. But that lemon-flavoured stuff was awful, it made me ill. I like the super-strength though. I'm hoping it will make me big and strong.'

'You're very small,' commented Mrs Stone. 'I'd always imagined vampires were big.'

'I know,' sighed Vlad. 'But I think all those years under the stone stunted my growth.'

'Have you tried furniture polish?' suggested Mrs Stone, her enquiring mind seizing the research possibilities.

'Never tried that,' said Vlad.

So Mrs Stone went and got a tin of lavender scented furniture polish. Vlad took it and put a bit on his finger and licked it.

'Ummm delicious,' he decided and ate the whole tin. As he scraped the last mouthful from the tin he asked. 'Did you make it yourself?'

'Well no,' said Mrs Stone a bit surprised. 'I buy it in a shop.'

'That's one of the things that's surprised me most about the twentieth century – the excellence of the things you can buy in the shops. I like shoe polish too. Judy gave me some for Christmas. Do they make *red* shoe polish?'

'No,' yelled Judy and Paul.

'Of course they do,' said Mr Stone. 'What are you two on about?'

'You don't understand,' explained Paul. 'Vlad goes a bit mad when things are red.'

'Yes,' confessed Vlad. 'Red rag to a bull, red blood to a vampire.'

'Oh, I see,' said Dad. 'Was that why there was all the red paint sprinkled in the class room today?'

'Yes,' said Vlad. 'I was very bad. Got 'cited you see.'

'And I suppose it was you who bit Gran and Aunt Margot and not the dog?'

Vlad nodded miserably.

'And was it you making a noise on the piano, so that people in the street kept asking me if I was composing music for a war film?'

Vlad nodded again.

'Well,' said Mrs Stone, 'I don't know what to say except that Vlad will have to go home – it was very unfair of you to bring him over in the first place – and he must go home as soon as possible.'

'Go home?' said Vlad. 'Yes, I'd like that, back to my mountains and the snow and the castles. Maybe I'd meet a lady vampire.'

'Don't you like it here with us any more, Vlad?' asked Judy.

' 'Course I do Judy,' answered Vlad. 'But there's no future for me here and I'll only go on getting you into trouble and anyway I am homesick for Transylvania.'

'And don't forget Judy,' went on Mrs Stone, 'once people know he exists, there'd be no peace ever again. There'd be reporters at the door every moment.'

Vlad's eyes lit up. 'Maybe I should stay,' he said, 'I'd be famous.'

'No, you must go back where you belong. It's cruel to keep you here. I admit I'd love to keep you – I'd be the most famous doctor in the world if I wrote a paper on vampirism from original research – but it wouldn't be fair.'

'However did you get out of Romania anyway, Vlad?' asked Mr Stone.

'I pretended I was a souvenir,' explained Vlad.

'I see,' replied Dad. 'Well I don't know how we're going to get you back. We'll certainly have to say that you don't exist. It was just a clever trick of Judy's in the classroom. They'll believe anything rather than that there was a real vampire in the school.'

'Not fair, want to be famous,' sulked Vlad.

'Well, you can't be,' said Judy. 'Dad's quite right. Miss Fairfax will believe me, if I say Vlad was just an action-man dressed up as a vampire. The children thought he was at our party.'

'Miss Fairfax'll think she only imagined she saw him flying when she came to from her fainting fit,' giggled Paul. 'She'll think she's mad.'

'That's enough, Paul,' interrupted Mr Stone, 'the poor woman's had quite enough trouble. I'll have to volunteer to help Judy clean up the classroom tomorrow.'

'Yes, let's concentrate on getting Vlad back to

Romania,' said Mrs Stone. 'I know, I've got an idea.'

'What's that?' said Vlad, who was beginning to like Mrs Stone as much as he liked her daughter.

'Well, there's a conference on blood circulation in Romania next month. I could try to get myself invited to that, and take you with me.'

Vlad went white.

'Good lord, what's wrong Judy, is he ill?' asked Mrs Stone.

'Can't bear blood, feel sick,' said Vlad.

Mr and Mrs Stone collapsed with laughter.

'Oh dear, what an amazing creature you are,' said Mr Stone. 'It sounds like a good idea though, darling, Romania, I mean. Can you take husbands along?'

'I don't see why I should, you never take me on your concert tours.'

'Here we go again,' laughed the children.

'What about me?' squealed Vlad, recovering from his fainting fit.

'It's all right, we're not laughing at you,' said Judy.

'I should think not,' said the vampire. 'Now, about this conference on the subject you mentioned.'

'Maybe I can cure you of your squeamishness, Vlad, and make you into a proper vampire, so that you live a normal life,' suggested Mrs Stone.

'Do you think you could? You must be a very clever doctor,' said Vlad. 'I always say to Judy that she must work hard at school if she wants to be clever like her mother.'

'I'm glad you try to get them to work hard,' said Mrs Stone.

'He doesn't,' said the children together indignantly.

'Come now children,' said Vlad. 'I've always said learning was a great thing. My Uncle Anatole was a famous vampire scholar and I'm always talking about him.'

'You are not,' said Paul. 'The only relative you ever even mentioned was Great Uncle Ghitza.'

'Anyway,' said Vlad, sitting happily on the arm of Mrs Stone's chair. 'How am I going to go home?'

'I could give you an injection and pretend that you were a specimen.'

Vlad turned pale.

'What's an injection?' he asked nervously.

'It's a prick with a needle that puts you to sleep.'

Vlad fell off the arm of the chair in horror.

'And what's a specimen?' he asked weakly.

'Oh, a dead animal you cut up to see what it's like inside.'

Vlad rolled under the chair.

'Vlad, what's the matter?' asked Judy, lying on the floor, so she could see Vlad cowering under the chair.

'That woman wants to vampirise me,' said the vampire accusingly. 'I'm not coming out till she promises not to use me as a specimen.'

'Don't refer to my mother as "that woman".'

'Well, she wants to vampirise me,' whimpered Vlad.

'Oh, don't go on,' said Paul.

'Listen Vlad,' said Mrs Stone soothingly. 'You can come out – I won't give you an injection – we'll think of something else.'

So Vlad came out and sat on Judy's knee looking balefully at Mrs Stone.

'Look Vlad, this is my medical bag,' said Mrs Stone. 'You could sit in there if you were very still.'

'What's a medical bag?' asked Vlad, who was still suspicious of Mrs Stone.

'It's the bag in which I keep all my instruments and pills and things to make people better,' explained Mrs Stone patiently.

'Let me see it,' said Vlad, standing on the edge and peering in. 'If I go in and investigate you won't close the bag?'

'No, I promise.'

So Vlad clambered into the bag and examined the contents. He took a swig from a bottle and pulled a face. 'Mm,' he said.

'I'm surprised you like that,' said Mrs Stone. 'It's disinfectant.'

Vlad found a pile of bandages and some cotton wool and began to pile them up.

'You don't have to go mad with the cotton wool,' said Mrs Stone.

'I'm making myself a bed,' explained Vlad and he lay down. 'Umm, it's very comfortable, I shall lie here and sleep all through the journey and no one will even suspect you've got a vampire in your bag.'

'I do hope you're right,' said Mrs Stone, 'but you mustn't drink my disinfectant.'

'What will you do when you get him back to Romania?' asked Mr Stone.

'Well,' said Mrs Stone. 'I've got an idea that might appeal to Vlad.'

The vampire perked up.

'I thought I'd take him along to the Minister of Tourism and suggest that Vlad fly around Count Dracula's castle and the tourists can film him and take photographs.'

'You mean be a film star?' asked Vlad wide-eyed. 'Caw, my dream come true – to think I came all the way to London to be a film star and I may end up being one on my very own doorstep. Caw! What sort of people will take all these pictures of me?'

'Tourists from all over the world – America, Australia, France, England, Japan, everywhere, and then when they get home on cold winter nights they'll show all their friends their films of you flying around the castle.'

'People in all those different countries will be looking at me?' said Vlad agog with amazement. 'Caw! Which is my better side?' said Vlad showing his two profiles, 'left or right?'

'They're both as ugly,' chided the children.

'You're just jealous, I'm going to be famous,'

yelled Vlad excitedly and he flew six times round the room, landed on the piano keys and began to run up and down.

Mr Stone grabbed him, 'Now stop that, you'll wake up the whole street.'

'Sorry,' said Vlad. 'Got 'cited you see.'

'Was it you at the football match?' asked Dad suspiciously.

Vlad nodded. 'Yes, I was very bad that day. Sorry, very sorry.'

'It's a bit late to apologize now after all the trouble you got Paul into. Sorry I took it out on you Paul,' said Mr Stone.

'Can Judy and me play you something on the piano?' asked Vlad who was anxious to change the subject. 'We've been practising.'

So Judy sat at the piano and Vlad stood on the keys and they began to play chopsticks together, Vlad jumping up and down and then hopping neatly from note to note as his contribution.

'Time for bed, all of you, now,' was Mr Stone's agonized reaction.

'Yes, off you go. We'll see if we can organize the Romanian trip, while you're in bed,' said Mrs Stone, and kissed all three of them. 'I never imagined being fond of a vampire,' she laughed.

Judy sadly put Vlad in his drawer.

'I'll miss you, Vlad,' said Judy.

'Miss you too, Judy,' agreed Vlad. 'But I've got to be a famous filmstar. It's my destiny.'

And as Judy was dropping off to sleep she could

hear Vlad's voice from the drawer singing:

'Oh Vlad the Drac,
He's going back,
He'd better pack,
Had Vlad the Drac,
Yes he's going back,
Is Vlad the Drac,
He's going back,
He's going back,
He's going back, back, back, back, back,
Is Vlad the Drac.'

10
Vlad Triumphant

The day came for Vlad's departure. Everything was packed and Vlad came downstairs on Paul's shoulder singing:

> 'Oh Vlad the Drac,
> He's going back,
> He's going back,
> Is Vlad the Drac.

'Come on everyone,' said Vlad. 'Join in my going-home song,' and Vlad conducted:

'Oh Vlad the Drac,' sang Mr Stone in a rich baritone.

'He's going back,' added Mrs Stone in her pleasant lilting voice.

'He's going back,' croaked Paul.

'Is Vlad the Drac,' finished Judy in a not too steady soprano.

'Now all together,' shouted Vlad and they all sang:

> 'Oh Vlad the Drac,
> Is going back,
> He's going back,
> He's going back,
> He's going back,

He's going back,
He's going back, back, back, back, back.'

'That was very good,' said Vlad.

'Now children,' said Mrs Stone, 'Dad and I think it would be better if you both said goodbye to Vlad here. If you come with us to the airport Vlad might do something silly.'

'Yes, might,' agreed Vlad. 'I'll be so sad to leave my friends, even Paul.'

'Now Vlad we've got to be sensible about this. Say goodbye quickly then into the bag with you. We'll all come to visit you in a year or so.'

'Before I get into the bag I've got to make my farewell speech,' said Vlad and he leapt on to the little platform at the foot of the banisters.

'Dearly beloved,' he began. 'We are gathered here today to say goodbye to Vlad the Drac, who after a brief stay in our island home, is returning to his homeland. All of us here I'm sure wish him every joy on his travels and much good fortune on his return. And yet is there a dry eye here as we comtemplate his departure, the departure of such a dear friend, no, more than a friend – a member of the family; who could know Vlad the Drac and not love him, who can remain unmoved by the thought that we may never be in his presence again? However, this is not the moment for selfish thoughts . . .'

'We'll miss the plane if he doesn't hurry,' muttered Mr Stone.

'He'll go on forever,' groaned Paul.

Vlad continued: 'Dear Friends, we must look to the future and think not of ourselves but of our dear friend . . .'

While he was still in full flood, Mr Stone crept up behind Vlad with a hat and held it over him until he stopped, wanting to be let out. 'How undignified,' was all the struggling vampire had a chance to say before Mr Stone transferred him to the bag. Then Mr and Mrs Stone rushed to the car and Judy and Paul stood on the pavement. As the car drove off Mrs Stone let Vlad out of the bag, and held him fast as he leaned out of the window.

'Bye,' he yelled. 'Bye Judy, bye Paul,' and he blew kisses.

'Bye Vlad, bon voyage – good luck,' shouted both the children and when the car was out of view they walked sadly back into the house.

'I will miss him, won't you Paul?' said Judy.

'Yes,' answered Paul putting his arm round her, 'but it was too much of a responsibility and it did mean we had to stay home a lot and worry all the time and it really wasn't fair to him.'

'I know,' said Judy. 'But I do love him, he was such a dear, funny little creature. I do hope he enjoys being a film star.'

'Yes,' said Paul, 'and maybe he will even manage to meet his lady vampire.'

When Mrs Stone returned from Romania she said the plan had gone well. The Minister of

Tourism had been very impressed by Vlad and had immediately offered him the post of resident vampire at Count Dracula's castle, with a lifetimes free supply of soap, washing up liquid, shoe polish or whatever he fancied. Vlad had seemed happy back in his old haunts, flying around in the snow and in the forest.

'I'm glad he's happy,' said Judy. 'Doesn't he miss us at all?'

'Of course he does,' said Mrs Stone. 'But don't worry, you'll see him again in two years' time. The Minister of Tourism is paying for us all to go and see him. Vlad insisted on it as part of the bargain. The Minister wants us to leave it for two years so that Vlad really settles down to his new job. Vlad told the Tourist Board that he wouldn't frighten one single tourist until the Minister agreed to our holiday.'

'Crafty old Vlad,' said Judy laughing.

So it was that two years later they were all sitting in their car driving through the very ravine where they had first met Vlad.

'That's where we found him,' shouted Judy, 'right over there near that tree.'

'That's right,' agreed Paul. 'His stone was under that tree.'

'We'll be seeing him soon,' said Dad as they drove on to Count Dracula's castle. They got out of the car and looked up at the dramatic turrets of the castle.

'I can't see Vlad,' said Judy in a disappointed voice.

Just then there was a flapping of cloaks and round the tower came seven vampires led by Vlad, turning and twisting just like the Red Arrows. Round and round they flew in different formations while tourists took photograph after photograph.

'I recognize Vlad,' said Paul, 'but whoever are the others?'

Just then Vlad spotted them and he flew down with delight.

'Hello, you've come to see me at last. Hello Judy, hello Paul, hello Mum and Dad, welcome to Transylvania.'

'Hello Vlad,' said Judy hugging him. 'Lovely to see you again, how are you?'

'Oooo I'm ever so well. May I introduce Mrs Vlad and my five children. They're called Judy, Paul, Mum, Dad and Ghitza.'

All the vampires smiled but said nothing.

'They don't speak any English,' explained Vlad.

The people taking the photographs began to mutter, wondering what the dangerous vampires were doing talking to tourists.

'I'll have to go,' said Vlad, 'my public you see, they love me and I mustn't be seen talking to you, it's bad for my scary image. You stay on and I'll see you when the performance is over.'

Every day, once an hour, on the hour, Vlad and his family flew round the castle, giving all the

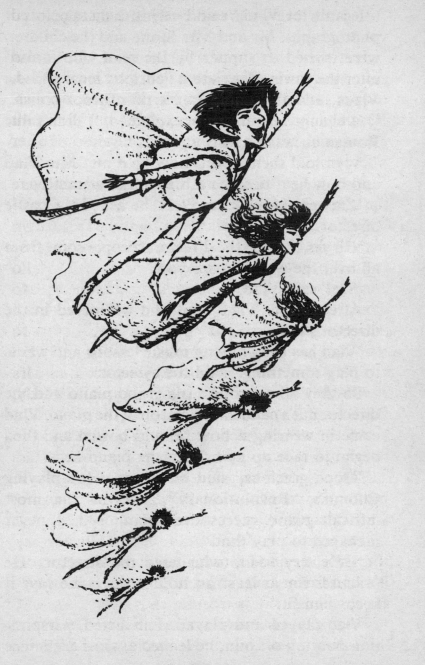

tourists a lovely scare and letting them take lots of photographs. Mr and Mrs Stone and the children were invited to supper by the man who looked after the castle. They ate a delicious meal and the Vlads sat with them eating a tin of floor polish.

'I changed my diet,' he explained. 'I didn't like Romanian washing-up liquid.'

Vlad told them about how he'd met Mrs Vlad and how he'd become a big tourist attraction.

'I'm very famous aren't I?' he asked the castle director.

'Oh yes,' agreed the director. 'People come from all over the world to see you.'

'See!' said Vlad.

After supper Vlad went and whispered in the director's ear.

'Vlad has been having music lessons and wants to play something,' said the director.

So they all sat round the grand piano and the director put a candelabra on top of the piano. Vlad came in wearing a bow tie and bowed and then began to race up and down the piano keys.

'Good gracious,' said Mr Stone. 'He's playing Chopin's "Revolutionary", one of the most difficult piano pieces ever composed. I never managed to play that.'

'He's very keen,' whispered the director. 'He practises for at least an hour a day – he says it keeps him fit.'

Vlad played and played. Exhausted, perspiration pouring off him, he leaned against the music

110

stand and panted: 'Now for my fifteenth encore.'

Paul groaned, 'He never did know when to stop.'

'Now Vlad,' said the director. 'You've played beautifully, but it's very late and our guests are tired and you'll be too exhausted to perform tomorrow if you go on.'

'But I like playing and I never had an audience for my music, only for being vampirish. Poor old Vlad, poor little Drac.'

'Are you still saying that?' asked Judy in amazement.

'Yes,' said the director, 'regularly – but no one takes any notice.'

'Before you send me to bed,' said Vlad, 'I've got to give that present I've been saving for my friend Judy.'

So Vlad took Judy off. He nibbled her ear affectionately.

'Wanted to see you on your own,' he said. 'I missed you, did you miss me?'

'Of course I did Vlad – I cried every night for weeks after you left.'

'So did I,' confessed Vlad. 'Everyone was very nice but I felt lonely, but then luckily the Minister of Tourism found me Mrs Vlad. See here's your present,' said Vlad proudly and handed Judy a tin of furniture polish and a photograph signed 'X-Vlad his mark'.

'I've been saving it up for months – wouldn't let any of the children touch it.'

'Oh, Vlad,' said Judy politely, 'how nice, just what I wanted.'

'I knew you'd like it – it's all for you. Don't give Paul any.'

'I won't,' said Judy. 'But Vlad fancy you having five children, I can't get over it.'

'Neither can I,' confessed Vlad. 'But they're nice aren't they?'

'Very nice,' agreed Judy. 'And it was good of you to call them after us.'

'Don't you think Paul junior is a bit cross-eyed?' said Vlad spitefully.

'No, he's lovely,' said Judy, 'all your children are lovely.'

'Well actually,' said Vlad. 'Just between the two of us, it's Ghitza that Mrs Vlad and I are worried about.'

'Why?' asked Judy.

'Well,' confided Vlad. 'He's showing dangerous signs of being just like his Great Uncle.'

'Oh dear,' said Judy horrified. 'Great Uncle Ghitza rides again.'

'Yes,' said Vlad with a mixture of pride and concern. 'I'm afraid so, he's going to be just like Great Uncle Ghitza – so people had better watch out people had! It's time for me to get some rest now. Bye Judy dear,' called Vlad and he flew off into the darkness. 'Don't forget to tell people they'd better watch out.'